Stealing Santa Rita

Stealing Santa Rita

Sherwood Stockwell

iUniverse, Inc.
New York Lincoln Shanghai

Stealing Santa Rita

iUniverse books may be ordered through booksellers or by contacting:

iUniverse
2021 Pine Lake Road, Suite 100
Lincoln, NE 68512
www.iuniverse.com
1-800-Authors (1-800-288-4677)

This is a work of fiction. All of the characters, names, incidents, organizations, and dialogue in this novel are either the products of the author's imagination or are used fictitiously.

ISBN-13: 978-0-595-39451-7 (pbk)
ISBN-13: 978-0-595-83848-6 (ebk)
ISBN-10: 0-595-39451-5 (pbk)
ISBN-10: 0-595-83848-0 (ebk)

Printed in the United States of America

1

MAY 13, 1988

Rubble rock bordered fingers of land that reached out to embrace the mile-long Santa Rita beach. Waves that were born far out in the Pacific rolled over the gently sloping sands whose multiple grains had drifted south from Mazatlan, the Sea of Cortez and points north in California. The waves continually rearranged the landform but they also provided the natural forces to help push Santa Rita's fleet of open skiffs up on the sand. The waves were god-sent locomotion for the fishermen who formed the backbone of this small Mexican *pueblo*.

Santa Ritans watched each morning for the arrival of the boats so that they could move from fisherman to fisherman to assess the previous night's catch. The residents were usually dispersed amongst the many skiffs to look and paw and bargain for the best *pesca,* but today they were concentrated around a single boat. Their typical purchasing zeal had been replaced by a concentrated curiosity. They were looking at a very dead body that had been placed on top of the day's catch of dorado, red snapper and ocean shrimp.

2

SEPTEMBER 13, 1968

Far to the north of Santa Rita, Pacific waves curled onto the coast at Santa Monica, California. This was the birthplace and home of Peter Oliver Sessions. His father, Peter Senior, had selected Santa Monica as a proper place to live for a man who had achieved a self-made success. Peter Senior was a costume designer and manufacturer for film studios in nearby Hollywood. The Sessions' home on La Mesa Drive carefully reflected the neighborhood Mission Style design theme and reinforced an order imposed on the street by a row of Moreton Bay fig trees. Their home was near the Riviera Country Club. Although being this close to the social hub pleased his parents, Peter would have preferred an address closer to the ocean. At an early age he was attracted to the surfing near the Santa Monica Pier and gradually worked his way south to bigger challenges in Ocean Park.

Ocean Park, labeled the Coney Island of the Pacific, was one of many amusement centers built in the late 1800's on California beaches. Ocean Park's original casino was purchased in 1891 by Abbot Kinney, an enterprising Easterner who had amassed a fortune producing *Sweet Caporal* cigarettes. Kinney bought additional acreage adjacent to the casino and on the 4th of July, 1905 he cut the ribbon to open a model city that in 1911 would be renamed the Venice of America. His development included a new huge pier where guests could visit a mammoth auditorium. Here they could listen to musical concerts and lectures by prominent performers who toured the popular Chautauqua circuit. The new town followed the design tenets of the *America Beautiful Movement*. Ornate "Venetian Renaissance" buildings like those around the original Plaza De San Marco bordered its main street, literally an extension of the pier. Its outstanding features were the manmade channels dug out of the lowland sand and clay. Here, ersatz gondolas echoed the picturesque activity of its namesake as they cruised along the new Venice's canals.

The extravagant concept began to fall apart. In 1920 most of Venice's two miles of canals were filled in, against the protests of local residents, and turned into paved roads that met the demands of the new automobile age. The focal point that once was called the Inland Lagoon became a giant traffic circle. In 1946 the Venice Pier was closed and by 1967 the amusement facilities of Ocean Park had lost their attraction and declared bankruptcy. The City of Los Angeles condemned and tore down 550 buildings and a 1970 major fire on the Ocean Park Pier was followed by 70 consecutive smaller fires set by transients.

This city of dreams became a place for those seeking their own kind of visions. The area was nicknamed Dogtown by the young, antisocial dropouts that camped in the ruins. They were the ones who torched the remaining timbers of the once magnificent playland at the beach. All that was left was The Cove, a stretch of beach sacred to surfers where high waves dashed between the remnants of the Pacific Ocean Park Pier. The average count was 10 waves every 15 minutes.

In Dogtown, Peter learned to hide his Brentwood area ties and gradually became somewhat accepted by the contra-mainstream youths, most of them the product of dysfunctional families. Peter's social acceptance was complete when he rode a dangerous wave through the small space between an upright piling from the old pier and its diagonal brace. After that he was invited to sit with the others and share tokes of marijuana as a participant in this "symbionic disharmony." After each had had their share of the weed, they drifted over to the Jeff Ho shop and bathed in imagined glow from the psychedelic colors and graffiti art designs on Jeff's surfboards.

Their next stop was the Tower Record shop to check out the 33-rpm releases. In many cases, owning the cover was more important than owning the music when it came to performers like The Who, Janis Joplin or the Grateful Dead. Each recording group had their own special designers to embody a message in the cover art. This double exposure to a new art field inspired Peter to think about following in his father's footsteps, albeit in a less respected area of design. He imagined the fun of creating record covers and surfboard designs and decided that his future lay with what he considered a more expressive art than making Hollywood costumes.

Upon graduation from high school, he enrolled at the New York Studio School on Williams Street in lower Manhattan to learn how to design consumer goods like custom tee shirts, music record sleeves and pulp magazine covers. During his first year Peter jumped into the challenges of using pencil and brush and developed a feel for both geometric and free form shapes. He was given occasional praise from instructors; but between the nightlife and participating in the antiwar demonstrations in Greenwich Village, Peter's studies suffered. When he finished the year with a 2.1 average and returned to Santa Monica, his father approached the problem directly.

"You can get the same flunking marks at a California college as you do at that expensive art school, and it wouldn't cost me half as much."

Peter Senior's edict would not just save money. California's higher education facilities were in fact catching up with eastern institutions in terms of academic achievement and faculty expertise. The post World War II slump in California's growth had been replaced with a population influx that required an expanded elementary, secondary and university system. Latter-day pioneers from the East were moving into the state to fill personnel gaps in a growing service sector. San Francisco was the financial center of the West and its port was filled with both passenger ships and freighters to serve the Pacific Rim. A fledgling collection of inventors, educators and financiers would soon make Stanford University the fountainhead of what would be called Silicon Valley. Further south in Los Angeles new factories and office buildings accommodated the new aircraft and electronics industries. All of this fueled a new economy with new tax receipts to pay for the new educational systems.

Legislators buoyed by the new coffers were eager to make good public education available to every state citizen. New revenues supported a spirit of optimistic growth that led to such phenomena as the existence on campus of three Nobel Prize winners at the University of California at Berkeley. This first campus of a university system was planned on a site that eastern landscapist Frederick Law Olmstead believed would accommodate any future student population. It was fast reaching its limit of physical growth. Similar problems were evident at UCLA in Los Angeles so the Regents of the University decided to build new campuses in Santa Cruz, Santa Barbara, San Diego and Irvine. The governor and legislature didn't stop there. They expanded what had been state colleges and called them California State Universities. It was a rewarding time to be an educator and an exciting time to be a student intrigued by campus activists. Every day proponents would gather near Sather Gate to campaign for Women's Rights, Free Speech and the end of the War in Vietnam.

His Father's edict was a compelling reason for Peter to reconsider California's educational and extracurricular opportunities. He was particularly attracted to the newly named University of California at Santa Barbara. Long a winter destination for affluent Easterners, Santa Barbara was noted for its avocados and famous for its landmark mission. This Queen of the California Missions was number ten in the chain envisioned by explorer and missionary Father Junipero Serra. His goal was to convert heathen Native Americans and cement Catholicism in the Spanish territories that were extending along the Pacific coast.

The Santa Barbara campus of a growing University of California was converted from a small teachers' college in 1944. UCSB seemed to fall academically in the middle of the University campus system. This made it quite accessible to enrolling student Peter Oliver Sessions. He was attracted by the slow scholastic pace and particularly by the university's location right on the Pacific Ocean. Peter began majoring in Business Economics as a favor to, or more accurately as an order from, his father. He gave him a choice:

"Get a degree or get a job!"

Peter chose the major that would assure him of a weekly allowance but he also padded out his schedule with Introductory Spanish.

The ocean waves meant surfing to Peter and riding the waves was a magnetic alternative to hanging out at the University Center or studying financial charts in his room at Anacapa Hall. Surfing was also an antidote to his frustration with women. He wanted their companionship but lacked experience on how to get there. He knew that motherly hugs were not the same as the male-female embraces he watched in the movies. He saw Ryan O'Neal make out with Ali MacGraw in *Love Story* but wasn't sure how he should make the first steps from simple friendship to those caring caresses. He was one of the few his age that didn't understand that sex in the '70s was just like buying new shoes. You kept trying them on until you found a pair you liked.

An urge to overcome his celibacy came one afternoon as he crossed the campus between Anacapa and the Physical Sciences building. A girl in a small group of sorority sisters must have had class schedules similar to his. Although he was a little put off by her height, he liked her golden hair, the way she wore a scoop neck tee shirt and the smooth glow of her skin that added mystery to the more obvious attributes.

He was surfing when he saw her again in a cluster of what he learned were Chi Delta Theta "sisters" walking along the beach. He was just about to dump his board and finish a run at Campus Point. He glanced up to see her, lost control and was flipped unceremoniously into the shallow water where waves turned to foam before rolling up on the sand. When he recovered his footing he tried to make light of it by going into what he hoped looked like the stance of a god from the sea. The other girls laughed at his pose, but she came over to ask,

"Are you sure you're O.K.? That looked dangerous."

"It's all part of the game," Peter replied. "You're nice to ask. What's your name?"

"Eugenia, but everyone calls me Genie."

"Do you surf? No? I can teach you."

Two days later, Genie showed up with another girl. They brought boards rented from a nearby surf shop. Peter didn't like the idea of teaching both of them, but that seemed the price he had to pay for knowing Genie. After the first day, what seemed like half the sorority house showed up at the beach to learn from "that cute guy". Soon, they were able to go out on their own and accept the challenge to their hairdos. He was left alone with Genie. He tried hard to conceal his interest and to keep his eyes away from the body hidden behind the two piece white bathing suit. Hoping that a joke would mask his eagerness, he said,

"I know I'm shorter than you are, but I'm broader so the differences equal out. Would you go out on a date with me?"

"You're nice, but I have to tell you that I'm already en......spoken for. You wouldn't want to tangle with him. He's a Marine."

Santa Barbara provided Peter with a sufficient buffer distance from his demanding parents, but was close enough so that he could borrow a family car on weekends. He also appreciated the security of his weekly allowance and the reward of an occasional home cooked meal. Despite all this, Peter Oliver Sessions was working towards a decision to change his lifestyle that was shared by many other male students his age. He saw little point in forever trying to please his father by studying for a career that didn't hold any interest.

Although there was talk that President Nixon might try to end the Vietnam War, he realized that leaving college could open the door to his being drafted. On the Santa Barbara campus going to Vietnam was about as popular with his friends as going into the family business. No one was that dumb. During a talk session of corridor mates, bolstered by puffs on a joint, the conversation turned to alternatives to the draft. Conscientious Objector? It would be hard to prove without a history of preaching pacifism. Escape to Canada? It was cold and too far from great waves. Mexico? There was an extradition treaty, but plenty of places to hide where living costs were low, Man, really low.

3

On a muggy afternoon, a '62 Willys Wagon traveling south from the United States turned left off Mexico 200 at the Santa Rita sign. The machine's rusting yellow body was divided into panels with raised ribs, a last echo of the wooden station wagon. At the lower right hand edge of the windshield was a faded decal touting the Huntington Beach Surfing Association, the honor badge of the vehicle's former owner. Two surfboards stuck out of a windowless rear end. The boards, a tent kit and a small duffel bag made up the total baggage of Peter Oliver Sessions. Peter slowed down as he left the asphalt paving and entered the dusty, cobbled access road. On his right was a small grove of banana trees. On the left, two grayish cows and a brown spotted horse, all skinny and never curried, pretended to enjoy their sparse grazing rights behind a two-row barbed wire barrier.

A few *Norte Americanos* preceded Peter to Santa Rita. They arrived to view a landscape where the green foothills of the Sierra Madre came down to the Pacific Ocean. A river from the mountains had created an alluvial plain as it made its way to the sea, and the land now held a small group of adobe houses. The new arrivals found a Santa Rita whose sheltered bay and easy access to the bountiful Pacific had for centuries supported a local fishing industry. As the industry grew, the village of Santa Rita became a transfer point between the sea and city fish markets. On its level lands a community grew, kept small and stable by its remote location within the surrounding jungle.

Peter had little appreciation for the extent of the tranquil scenery, nor did he know that his destination was named for Margarita of Cascia also known as "*Rita La Abogada de Imposibles.*" Rita lived in the 14th Century. Her tortured life witnessed the murder of an abusive husband and the death of her twin sons. Sainted as an Advocate of the Impossible, Santa Rita was a patron of those with desperate causes. They would journey great distances to ask for the saint's blessings.

Peter was also unaware that his trip south had paralleled the water route originally taken by the explorer Juan Rodriguez Cabrillo in 1542. Cabrillo, a Portuguese citizen paid by the Spanish to do their dirty work, departed from the nearby port of Natividad, later known as San Blas, Mexico. He sailed north to explore the coast and finally discovered what is now the State of California. Unfortunately, he forfeited the joys of fame and accolades by dying before the return trip.

Peter might have imagined himself a similar explorer, but instead of looking for gold his quest was to find an ideal spot to use the surfboards in the Jeep Wagon. To him the surfboards were unrivaled instruments of pleasure. He was a devotee of the sport first championed by Hawaiian Duke Kahanamoko in the 1920s that had been adopted by hundreds of 1970 adventurers that sought an Endless Summer wherever the call, "Surf's up!" beckoned.

Peter headed into a village that was remote, even though less than thirty miles from the city of Mazatlan as the *pelicanos* flew. People traveled the two lane road, officially Mexico Route 200, through villages where palm-thatched stands along the road sold local fruits, grilled chickens and barbequed oysters. Drivers knew that they'd arrived at Santa Rita when they reached the small bull ring. From the *plaza de toros* a road paved with river rock passed by a collection of abandoned military barracks before it wound across a bridge. The barracks and the cobbled stones were all that remained of the era of El Presidente Manuel Juarez. He used Santa Rita as a summer capital. That is, until he was indicted for fraud. Some say the indictment was an amazing political coup, for no one dared accuse a governmental official of impropriety in those days.

The road from highway 200 became *Independencia* when it entered the town proper. Travelers first passed by four different grocery shops or *tiendas*. Each hung flyspecked bananas, pineapples and corn tassels along their fronts. Between the shops were the Santa Rita Café, the Michoacán Ice Cream Parlor and the *Ferreteria*, a hardware and building supply store. *Independencia* ended at the *Plaza Central* which became a unifying hub for all the roads that converged there with haphazard alignments. A small church dedicated to the patron saint fronted on the Plaza, opening its carved wooden doors on Sunday to welcome most of the villagers for Mass. The white plastered structure supported a modest bell tower that daily rang out the time at fifteen minute intervals but clanged in double time on Sabbath mornings.

Across the Plaza from the church, signs on a taco stand announced a choice of fillings: *pollo,* grilled chicken, or *carne,* a generic term for anything that walked on four legs. One hoped that Santa Rita dogs were not included, because every block of the dusty streets held a half dozen mongrels of indefinable origin. Each mutt selected the closest post possible to passing traffic so that the vehicular dust would help ward off the insects that were also permanent residents of Santa Rita.

The town became communally owned after the Mexican Revolution in 1916 when the revolutionary government decreed that the large Spanish land grants would be given back to the *campesinos* or farmers. The communities thus established were called *Ejidos* and they were controlled by Ejido councils. Within the Ejido, dwellings were randomly erected on communal open spaces. Along central village streets, gaps between buildings were progressively filled to provide continuous walls punctuated by entry doors. In the wealthier Mexican cities, the doors in similar street side walls opened to lush courtyard gardens. In Santa Rita they opened directly to living spaces. No one could afford the luxury of a landscaped entrance.

A single north-south road connected the Plaza and the beach. Santa Ritans lacked a frontage road in the other direction along the oceanfront. They just used the beach as their circulation route. Few residents owned the automobiles that might have used a road, and the Ejido council rejected any proposals for constructing anything permanent along a waterfront that was ever threatened by the high waves of October storms.

A few restaurants along the beach front served meals under inexpensive *palapas* whose palm frond roofs shielded diners from the hot sun. Here locals and a few tourists looking for an "authentic" vacation experience enjoyed fresh fish grilled on a mesquite open fire. They scooped up *guacamole* made from local tomatoes, onions and avocados and spread it on *tostadas*. These were *tortillas* made in the factory near the Plaza and fried into crispy strips. Tortillas were such a basic staple that their price was set by the federal government at 3 pesos per half kilo. Santa Ritans could enjoy a diet of seafood caught nightly under the torchlight from the skiffs that fished near offshore reefs. The catch was accompanied by fruits and vegetables that grew beside the ordered rows of corn stalks planted in the productive valley lands along the river.

Peter parked the Willys near the Plaza and walked the short distance to the beach. The only things that interrupted his view of the water's edge were white and blue boats that had been pulled up above the high tide line. He took off his

Bass Weejuns and walked barefooted down the sand to his left. From the angle of the sun, he guessed that he was heading west and that the beach itself faced due north. He soon arrived at a point where the land formed a curving, rocky arm that sheltered three more boats moored to floating plastic gallon jugs. Here the terrain sloped sharply upwards. High above the beach, he spotted what looked like a half finished building sitting in the middle of a grassy meadow.

He turned around and continued his walk to the other end of the beach where he found more rocky shore. When his inspection was complete, he stopped at a beachside restaurant, sat on a paint-splattered chair with a well-worn, woven seat and looked at the grease stained menu. It was stacked between red and green Tabasco bottles sitting on the oilcloth table. After ordering a *Chile Relleno* and *Pacifico* beer, he considered his next move. He might pitch his tent on the beach or in the jungle fringes at the east end of the beach, but there would be an advantage to being higher up where he could look down on the ocean and be isolated from possibly threatening storms.

When the waiter brought his food, Peter attempted a conversation and found that the Mexican was eager to talk about the town. His Spanish was interspersed with English learned during work as a short order chef across the border in El Paso.

   "*Si, Señor, la aldea es pequeño......* small, Senor. We are small."

Talk turned to the layout of the town and eventually to the half finished palapa that Peter had noticed on the west end of the beach.

   "*La lamarmos La Casa de Cabra.*"

He explained that the locals called it the House of Goats because whoever built it had disappeared and now only the goats grazed there. Peter wasn't worried about the goats. He knew that he had found a spot to pitch his tent.

4

Peter Oliver Sessions drove his Willys Wagon west from Santa Rita's plaza. The road soon narrowed into two ruts as it started up a hill, passing a compound surrounded by a high, white stucco wall. This was the town's fish processing center. Passers by could hear the low drone of the compressor that refrigerated fish not sold on the beach. It was kept here until the arrival of the daily pick-up truck from Mazatlan. A few small houses across the road were variously colored in the only blue, yellow and green paints carried in the Ferreteria. The houses thinned out as Peter passed into the jungle lands outside of town. He soon reached another turn-off that he hoped would lead to the Casa de Cabra. As he rounded the crown of a hill he could see where trees had been cut to open the site to a 180 degree vista of the beach below. Peter stopped the Willys at the edge of the open space and got out to set his first footsteps on "Goat House" land.

A raised brick platform constructed from local red *ladrillos* stood at the ocean side edge of the clearing. At some points, solid walls had been started on the platform. Their random tops suggested that the builder had been suddenly stopped by a fatal illness or, more likely, had simply run out of money. A tent-like palapa had been built on a portion of the platform. Peeled tree trunks were bound together at their tops and connected at intervals by horizontal sticks. palm fronds were tightly laced between the horizontals to provide a rain-resistant shelter.

Pulling his tent kit out of the wagon, Peter looked for the best spot to establish a campsite. He found a level area with a great view of the ocean that was set far enough back from the edge to keep his activity hidden from the beach below. He spread out a groundsheet and began pounding in stakes to hold down the tent corners.

"What do you do that for?"

Peter turned around to see a well-tanned, long-haired youth that was a head taller and some forty pounds heavier than he was.

"I was told this was not private land. I want to camp here!" answered Peter who then sagely added "…….for a few days."

"No, what I want to know is why do you pitch that tent when there is plenty of room under the palapa?"

He pointed towards the structure.

"Name's Rostovitz. They call me Rusty. What's yours?"

Peter hesitated, wondering how best to camouflage his Santa Monica labels. He wanted to fit in with this new community and finally settled upon a seldom-used nickname.

"My name is…….Pedro! What have you got inside that grass shack?"

Rusty directed him to the palapa. It was closed on most of its perimeter but open to the ocean on the north side. He pointed out the water supply (a hose bibb) and his sleeping area.

"The bathroom is all natural! Just get far enough from here to keep the flies away. You can build a divider over there under the palapa and make it a two bedroom kind of place."

Rusty led him to an open area near some cardboard boxes. Pedro guessed that these were Rusty's storage trunks. Three surf boards leaned against the palapa walls, their bottoms resting on a floor of flat paving stones and sand. There were no light fixtures or other apparent signs of electricity.

Rusty Rostovitz told Pedro that he had come to Santa Rita from Gary, Indiana, the previous year. He grew up in Gary, learning to fight all there was to fight in a once vibrant steel mill town that was slowly dying as production moved overseas. Rusty had a tough immigrant father, lived in a tough neighborhood, attended a tough parochial school and faced all the problems of a decaying city once domi-nated by a single industry. Rusty beat them all. He fisted his way to respect amongst his peers, captained the school football team and soaked up knowledge of the outside world from the priests and nuns.

Rusty described his stand on Vietnam. He was not afraid of the physical side of waging a war. He enjoyed a fight and didn't want to become a Conscientious Objector or head north for sanctuary in Canada. As one of six Rostovitz children, however, he had been lectured daily by his parents about the plights of labor versus management. They said that the rich dominated the poor and that factory owners only wanted a war so that they could make profits from the sale of weapons. Rusty wanted no part of a war that he believed would primarily benefit Capitalists. He wasn't going to be sucked into Lyndon Johnson's mistaken invasion of a far-removed nation. Rusty quietly disappeared.

Drifting from job to job he made his way south, finally crossing the border in Nogales. Once in Mexico he was isolated from the events of the outside world and with simplistic logic made his struggle for survival an honorable pursuit. He found other Americans with similar views and listened to their stories of welcomed refuge in the coastal villages. Arriving in Santa Rita he made an effort to become a friend of all those around him and especially enjoyed the camaraderie of his newfound sport of surfing.

In a way, Rusty's outgoing nature was a perfect counter to Pedro's introverted character. Peter Oliver Sessions had inherited a taciturn temperament. He was not going to tell Rusty that he also suffered from what the medical profession would later define as ADD, or Attention Deficit Disorder. He could not stick with any task more complex than tying his shoes and disliked the confinement of a classroom. With any kind of project that required putting things together, Peter would not read the instructions or take offered advice. When the scattered parts would not fit together, he would internally freeze and leave them in disarray.

Peter eventually found an escape from his conflicts with the soothing solace of the ocean waves. There, only one element surrounded him and he relaxed in its rhythms. As he grew, his surfing became his physical and mental protection from the outside world, even when his parents insisted that he learn a more socially acceptable sport. They urged him to take advantage of the tennis courts at the club. This, they hoped, would counter what they saw as a diffidence growing out of his association with those Hippies from Ocean Park. He made this concession to them, but slowly turned tennis into a game of retaliation. His frustration from a serving or playing mistake was forgotten when he made a shot that his opponent could not return. He loved making a tricky cut shot that landed close to the net when his opponent was still on the back line. He covered his treachery with a straight faced apology.

"Oh, my grip slipped. So sorry."

Many of his difficulties might have been minimized with a good sense of humor, but unfortunately Peter had none, particularly when it came to laughing about himself. The closest he came to smiling was when he was on a surfboard where he could compete with the ocean without having to mingle with his peers.

5

The morning sun eased over a coastal spur of the *Sierra Madre Occidental* and began to light up *Bahia Santa Rita*. From the northwest, waves with a two to three foot crest moved across the shallow bay to break onshore. Like players carrying their instruments onstage for a symphony concert, surfers with their boards sauntered onto the beach. Singly or in small groups they entered the water and swam seaward. They seemed to know just where they belonged on this giant stage as they spread out in ordered lines along the arc where waves began to crest.

Rusty and Pedro made the short trip down the slope from the Casa de Cabra and walked along the sand. When they met a cluster of surfers still onshore, Rusty hailed each one by name and then headed for the center of the beach to catch the best waves. Pedro kept on the edge of the group watching it grow to a dozen or more people.

They were all dressed in the uniform of the day: a tattered tee shirt printed with nihilistic slogans draped over swimming jams that hung to the knees. Although the surfers might pick tee shirts off any rack with slogans that changed from day to day, their trunks were special equipment. A few had on cotton shorts in faded Hawaiian prints, purposely oversized to protect against exposure. Here and there were some Turtle Kings and Wave Wears on the California expatriates. The more experienced surfers wore nothing but industrial grade canvas shorts made by loving beach mothers with double stitching and special pockets for wax. The shorts had to be tough because they were lived in, worn all day long.

Santa Rita drew the extremists that wanted to spend a lifetime of unscheduled days in an affordable place with awesome waves. In Pedro's group there were a few men in their forties with regulation long hair and unkempt beards and a few mature women who hid their two-piece Catalina suits under the tees and jams. Amongst the mostly white surfers were a few dark tanned Mexicans.

Some of the cluster dropped to their knees to add slickness to the bottom of their boards. Each lovingly applied their own special formula based on bee's wax, ski racers' wax or even Turtle Car Wax.

Pedro could see a cross section of surfing history written in the boards gathered along the beach. The older men were still using long boards made of balsa wood wrapped in fiberglass. Others had 8 to 9 feet tall Standard Malibu boards with the fiberglass applied over a foam core interior. The newest boards were shorter, only 6 to 7 feet long, carrying labels of their manufacturers: Infinity, White Kite or Twin Fin. Each maker produced boards with an identifiable shape and their own special tail fins. The signature of the board's manufacturer was as important to its owner as that on a golf club, baseball glove or tennis racquet.

The boards became shorter with an increasing knowledge of hydrodynamic principals but the biggest change in their design owed its genesis to a manufacturing mistake. At the time, all the boards were either cigar-shaped or wider in the front than the back. A steering fin on the back end helped keep the board on track. One day a helper in a Venice surfboard shop accidentally glued the steering fin on the wide front end of a board he was making. After laughing off the mistake, the shop owner took what became known as his pig board to the beach for an experimental run. Whereas conventional surfers always nose rode with their weight up front, the shop owner found that his reject board turned beautifully if he placed his weight on the back of the board.

Pedro had learned all this by following Malcolm Gault-William's web page, *Legendary Surfer*. *It described* how the wide back idea lay dormant until an Australian named Nat Young appeared at the third World Surfing Championships in San Diego. He excited the spectators with his own version of the pig board. While the others were using their boards as a platform for maneuvers, the Australian seemed to use his board to attack, riding the waves in places that others never had. Gault-Williams quoted a competitor named Mike Doyle:

> "While we were riding long, straight cigar boards, Nat's board was much more suitable for doing cut backs and what I call S-turn surfing. Nat gave us a lesson in the future of surfing. While we would cut back or stomp on the tail to stall, Nat would cut back by compressing his body and pushing out with his legs, driving to get more power off his fin. He came out of a turn with more power than when he went into it, which allowed him to keep the board moving all the time, cutting a much bigger pattern in the water."

The then Peter Sessions had been at the World Surfing Championships and remembered that the waves at Ocean Beach were unusually small that day. This didn't keep Nat Young from carving all over them. Pedro thought about the event as he paddled out and took up a position on the edge of the pack, sitting astride his Jeff Ho Zephyr board. He looked out to sea, waiting for the highest wave of a set to approach. Then he extended his arms to lift his body into a crouch on the board. The board moved with the wave. When it crested Pedro felt the thrill of momentary weightlessness as he was carried forward by the tremendous natural force. The three steps were accompanied by a singsong mantra for each phase of the action. It sounded like "Oli...Ola.... Olé! As each new wave was conquered, his confidence improved and he moved closer to the center of the group, mouthing" *Oli.Ola, Olé,* "with each successful pass.

Finally reaching Rusty, he stayed in the center with him for the morning.

Around noon the orchestrated line began to fold as each surfer headed in for lunch. Rusty and Pedro headed for a palapa with white painted walls emblazoned with a 2 foot high blue Corona logo. They ordered fish tacos and Pacifico beers, leaving the Corona for the tourists. Munching a fried tortilla chip dipped in hot salsa, Rusty asked,

"What the hell were you shouting out there?"

"It's my salute to a good run. Oli!. Starts me off. Ola' as I catch a good wave, 'Olé' as sort of a bravo as I move into a crouch and start a good run. I'm not sure what it all adds up to."

"What's with the Oh-lie? Is that your nickname?"

"No, and it's Aw-li. No one ever calls me that except my mother. It's short for her maiden name of Oliver. It's my middle name. I would never know you were talking to me. Let's stick with Pedro."

That evening, Rusty grilled some *Dorado* and potatoes over an open fire. When Pedro tipped over the coffee pot by mistake, Rusty derided him.

"Watch your clumsy feet....OHLIE!" He knew it made Pedro mad and only used the nickname to taunt him. Gradually, others would pick up the word, but only use it when they wanted to refer to Pedro's introspective stance or as sort of an "in" joke. Rusty wanted to smooth over the rift he'd created during the meal and said,

"Let's go down to the village and check the action." Heading for Ramone's, they passed a group partying on the front porch of a large house on Independencia. Rusty hailed the apparent host, "*Hola Juan. Que Pasa?*"

"My friend, Rusty, please come in to the party! Also, your *Amigo!*"

Rusty and Pedro moved onto the porch and Rusty began introductions.

"This is Pedro. You saw him take the high ones today."

"*Esta Pedro, mi amigo.*"

Pedro could recognize some of the surfers he'd seen that morning. Some were drinking beer, some smoking weed, a few munching tostadas. He drifted towards a boy and girl that were engrossed in a discussion. The girl spoke.

> "But you've got the dates all wrong. Kerouac wrote *On the Road* in 1949 and it wasn't published until 1957. Keysey didn't get *Over the Cuckoos Nest* out until '62."

She had a head of hair still wet and stringy from an afternoon's surfing. She wore cutoff jeans and a clinging cotton top with obviously nothing between the cotton and her prominent nipples.

> "You're probably right. Maybe I' m confusing it with the cross-country bus trip. At Stanford, there was a teacher last year named Robert Stone who had just returned from Nam as a war correspondent. He told us about Keysey painting up an old bus and driving it from California to the New York World's Fair with a load of bombed friends. They stopped at Kerouac's and he got really pissed off at the mindlessness of the whole thing. Funny, Stone talking about the stoned."

> "You had Stone too? I had him, I think, at Irvine, or maybe UCSD. I moved around a lot. All Stone could talk about was his book, *A Hall of Mirrors* and how it was going to make him a shitpot full of money when he sold the movie rights. I think that Paul Newman tried to pull it off, but the movie stunk. Too bad, because Stone needed to support a big habit."

He tried again to make up for his mistake about the dates.

"You know Keysey was here in Mexico in 1966? In Manzanillo. Before going back and giving himself up to the San Mateo police"

He couldn't remember why Keysey had to surrender, so offered her a toke on his half finished marijuana.

"And Kerouac covered it all in *Lonesome Traveler*. Remember the bit about No-gales?"

She shook her head.

Pedro turned to see Juan heading his way. Juan was a head taller and had a swarthy complexion compared with Pedro's towhead and fair skin. Juan put an arm around Pedro's shoulder and gently hugged him questioning,

"Would you like some first class Acapulco Gold? Mexican Green? No seeds in my cannabis. You name it, Juan has *mucho!*"

Pedro remembered the trade language on the Dogtown beach. Acapulco Gold was great stuff and Mexican Green so precious that no one had ever smoked it. He shook his head.

"I'll just start with a beer. Thanks, anyway."

He slowly removed himself from Juan's arm and moved to find Rusty to ask,

"What gives with Juan?"

"Ah, Juan. Juan is our entrepreneur. While we do our best to stay alive on a few coins, he is becoming rich on our habits. Let me tell you about Juan. Here is a kid that grew up on the streets of Mexico City. He is a true *Mestizos*: some native Indian from way back, some Spanish in his mother, some Jewish from his father. They sent him out to hustle Chiclets to tourists at the age of six!

He graduated to jumping on car hoods at street intersections at the age of eleven, offering a windshield wash from a spray bottle for a peso a shot.

In Santa Rita, he is a mule for the syndicate. He used to carry hash across the border until Nixon began to crack down with his War on Drugs and practically closed the Tijuana crossing for three whole weeks. Juan just made it by outrunning a Narco agent. Now, he's lying low here where there's no local police. Buy from him but watch your ass."

Pedro went for a beer and tried to find the braless girl with the wet hair. She and her friend had left the party.

6

Back in the United States, bitterness against the Vietnam War was increased with the killings of 4 student demonstrators at Kent State by National Guardsmen. It simmered down after President Richard Nixon ordered the withdrawal of all the American troops. Any popularity that Nixon gained by the order was quickly quashed by a Republican attempt to burglarize Democratic headquarters in Washington's Watergate building. Nixon mistakenly denied any involvement in the historic heist and this error finally led to his resignation. In Santa Rita the expatriates began to look for news of some kind of pardon that would allow them to return to the States. Of course, any such news was coming in piecemeal to Santa Rita and it might be overshadowed for surfers by the local weather report.

The Mexican government was going through its own upheaval. The lavish expenditures of Luis Echeverría had led to a sixty percent drop in the value of the peso. His financial exploits were equaled by the new president, López Portillo. Portillo went on a spending binge fueled by the billions that were flowing into the treasury from oil sales by the nationalized Pemex Corporation. Portillo borrowed to build public infrastructure and subsidize consumer goods. This worked until an international oil surplus caused a cut in barrel prices. Portillo tried to buck the trend. He ordered Pemex to raise prices and threatened to cut off any consumers that would not meet Mexican oil prices. Consumers soon went to other, cheaper producers. The enormity of the accrued Mexican debt forced the exchange rate for the peso to again drop, this time by almost two hundred percent.

Most Gringo surfers in Santa Rita were numb to such national and international problems. Of course they were happy that the peso drop made dollars from home buy many times what they did before devaluation; but the more important thing each day was how the Pacific waves were breaking upon Santa Rita shores. Each wave also brought ashore a few grains of sand that were carried by the littoral drift that constantly swept the coast from north to south. In turn, grains left Santa Rita to build up beaches at points below. Sometimes the movement of the grains of sand was echoed by the procession of surfers from the states. They would drift into Santa Rita and then move on with their boards to another beach, another set of waves and another party.

Pedro's money began to run out. He rummaged through his duffel bag to see if he'd missed any small coins. There was a bank savings book showing his final $100.00 withdrawal. There was also a picture of his mother that he kept because she seemed to be the only one to understand his desire to escape. She had given him two $20.00 bills as he left the house. The $140.00 had gone towards gas, oil and the necessities of survival: beer, pot and tacos.

On one of their daily trips to the beach, Pedro casually told Rusty,

"I need some money. My fortune has run out."

"Yeah, I could use some too. Let's think about it. The quickest way is dealing drugs, but there are too many others doing the same thing. There's no way we'll beat out the locals for restaurant or beach-boy jobs. They still don't like us much here, at least not enough to pay us anything."

Walking along the sand, they passed two Huichols that had come from their Sierra Madre village to try and sell their few handicrafts to the foreigners. The Indians were dressed in their native costumes of white cotton decorated with colored bands at the bottoms of their sleeves, shirts and pants. One held out a small square towards Pedro. Its geometric design was woven from colored beads and looked to Pedro as if it might be some kind of religious symbol.

The other Indian held a larger "painting" made from colored yarn. In broken Spanish he described his picture of the Huichol world. The center was planted with the seeds of fruits and plants to sustain life. Above the center he pointed to a Deer Person that was the soul of the gods. He showed Pedro a *Kawi* worm and an *Iguana* lizard. The two Norte Americanos learned then that the Kawi was an edible delicacy and the Iguana represented food for future, unborn Huichols.

Rusty got more interested in the Huichol world when he learned that Peyote was used during religious ceremonies. He voiced what he hoped was a sage opinion,

"We should be able to use these guys somehow."

Pedro responded.

> "I like the designs. I like the workmanship. Why don't we act as go-betweens and sell the Indian stuff to tourists?"

By asking around at the restaurants and shops, they learned that the Indians lived in a remote mountain valley to the southeast of Santa Rita. It could not be too far away because the Huichols walked the distance between the two points. Apparently, the Indians did not see many visitors and had their own native tongue. A few of them spoke some Spanish.

Rusty and Pedro knew they needed to build a relationship with the Indians. The next time that they saw the Spanish-speaking Huichol, whose name was roughly translated as José, they pooled a few pesos and purchased one of the beaded squares. Over a period of months the trust barrier between the two surfers and the two Indians was removed and gradually the Gringos convinced Jose that they should become his sales agents. Part of the agreement with Jose was that they would be allowed to visit his hometown in order to meet the crafts people and better understand how things were made. An invitation was finally offered to them.

Pedro drove Rusty in the Willys. They were heading north to Jose's home.

> "Are we sure this is a good idea, Rusty? I mean going into a strange place in the jungle where nobody speaks English?"

> "It's safer than being in the muck in 'Nam."

> "Do you ever worry or feel guilty about not being there?"

> "When that asshole Nixon admits how bad things were, he'll be happy he's saved a few guys like us." Rusty then added, "Look at what happened in France, 1918, 1944. With all the men dead in the war there was no sex for women, no new voters to keep electing guys like Tricky Dick!"

After passing through La Rosa they looked for a road heading east. Jose had described a square stone structure sitting on a hilltop about a mile from the main road. They turned on a secondary road just beyond this landmark. The land along the road had been cleared and planted with banana trees whose beauty would be short lived. As soon as they produced a harvest they died off to be replaced with another food crop.

The rutted road soon brought them to a split that presented three possible routes. They could go straight ahead, go through a cattle gate that closed off a road parallel to the road they were on or take a hard right. Jose's directions had been scant. They tried the straight-ahead route for another mile until it turned into a rocky, rutted pathway. They turned around and headed back.

Rusty suggested that they should take the road to the hard right that seemed to be headed for the river valley. Jose had described the stream as one of the inspirations to their artwork. The new route took them down to a dry riverbed bordered by a barbed wire fence. They parked the car under a tree, walked through a pedestrian opening in the fence and started out on foot down a well-trodden path beside the riverbed. Soon the jungle pathway, cool under the dense tree canopy, led through a rocky moraine left by years of flooding. The large gray granite boulders had been rounded off by centuries of exposure to the river that raged through there during heavy rains. The two men exchanged excited comments.

"Look! There are markings on these rocks. They must have been here for a long time. They were carefully chiseled out to form some kind of symbols."

"Here is a cross. Do you suppose this was Spanish?"

"There, a figure that might be a man." Its head looked like a straw broom and the body was made up of three squares inscribed with circular spirals.

They reached a spot where the river became a waterfall during storms. It had carved out a cliff that Rusty estimated to be thirty feet high. The years of wash had cleaned out softer horizontal and vertical bands of rock. This made the solid cliff walls look like they were made of huge, nearly-square, boulders that were randomly stacked on top of each other. Nature had carved away three larger recesses that Pedro guessed might be used as alters for religious offerings.

Their path led around and up above the cliff. Soon it opened to a large meadow-like clearing that was rimmed by dwellings. Some were made of stone but most were simply palm-frond palapas. A few Huichols looked out of their doorways at them but made no sounds of welcome. One called out a command and soon Jose appeared. Rusty started to speak.

"Jose, this is wonderful. You have a *Paradisio*. Tell us about the carvings on the stones. Are those Catholic crosses?"

"They are made by our ancestors who came here long before the Spaniards. No one has been able to interpret them, but we know they had religious meaning. Those that came before we Huichols were called Throat Cutters. They captured and then sacrificed children of rival tribes as an offering to the gods for good rains, sunshine and bountiful crops. Jose laughed.

"Be careful so that you do not become a sacrifice."

"Do you...do you still....do that?"

"No. We are from a different branch of the old tribe, but some of their dances and ceremonies have survived. I know that you would like to see one."

Although the two surfers thought they had maneuvered Jose into the new association, it wasn't all one-sided. Jose could see that both he and the village could benefit from having a Gringo representative. He had picked this day for their visit in order to impress them with an important Huichol event. First, he wanted to introduce them to the village arts.

The Indian artifacts that were being sold in Santa Rita were part of a history handed down from generation to generation. The Huichols had no written records of their ancestry. They were in the Sierra Madre Mountains when the Spanish first arrived in Mexico in 1531. Some think they were a branch of the Aztecs, driven into the mountains to escape attacks by other tribes. In their remoteness, they had retained their own language and art forms and a pantheistic religion that embraced a balanced natural world. Their worship was not to any god, but to the sun and rains that were critical to producing crops and to the rivers, rocks and wildlife that surrounded them. They saw themselves as keepers of the Earth and called themselves "Healers." Their bead and yarn paintings described the order of a natural world symbolized by the animals, plants and trees that they saw around them.

While the Mexican government was encouraging tourism as a source of income for the natives, religious reformers were trying to convert them to Christianity. Despite the attempt to change their faith, the Huichols knew that tourists with money to spend would be attracted to their celebration of the sacred cactus, *Peyoti*. Jose wanted the Peyote ritual to be the high point of his new representatives' visit.

Prior to the ritual, a shaman of the tribe had led a dozen villagers to San Luis Potosi, far northeast of the Sierra Madres, in order to hunt for the sacred plant. Along the route the shaman or *mara'akame* coached the group of pilgrims in a confession and purification ritual as preparation for their visit to an earthly Paradise. Upon arrival, the shaman told stories that had been passed down from generation to generation about the spiritual powers of Peyote. The hunt began. After sufficient plants were harvested, the group returned to the village to share their bounty.

Now their efforts were being celebrated. Jose led his companions to the edge of a cleared opening in the jungle to watch the event. A group of men and women formed a large circle with each of them doing a loosely coordinated ritual dance step. In the middle of the circle sat an instrumentalist and song-leader whose monotone chanting marked time for the dancers. Containers filled with wine or the milk of the Peyote plants were placed around the circle. Occasionally one or two dancers would stop to refresh themselves. Their gap in the dancing circle was quickly closed and the circumambulation continued. After watching for a while, Jose pulled the Gringos away.

> "This ceremony will go on all day and night until everyone is exhausted. It is not proper to watch too long. This is a healing, a religious ceremony that goes back for three thousand years. During the dance my people receive visions of the past that put them in balance with the earth and all other living things. I cannot explain more."

The ritual dancing may have impressed Pedro, but Rusty could only think of all that peyote. Back in the States, he'd heard about the psychedelic drunks and the great highs from Mexican peyote. Perhaps he'd found the right place.

7

After a year of hawking Huichol artifacts on the dusty *Independencia,* Pedro and Rusty expanded their sales to include small, clay figurines and cameos of ancient Mayan idols. These had been dug, albeit illegally and secretly, from the hillside grave sites of the Huichol tribe. This kind of plundering was taking place in many parts of Mexico because the federal and local governments turned a blind eye to the historical importance of the materials being carried off. Some went to Mexican museums but most to living room shelves in other countries.

While their income was sporadic, their sales effort gave Pedro and Rusty daily contact with an expanding tourist trade. They found that many visitors complained about attacks of *Tourista.* This twenty-four hour agony of stomach pains and uncontrollable excretion typically resulted from meals prepared under less than sanitary conditions by the street food vendors. There had to be a better approach to serving healthy, palatable cuisine.

Rusty and Pedro made a deal with the owner of a small house facing the plaza. The owner's family was moved inward and a new sign was painted on the wall facing the street to announce the *Casa de Tacos.* Pedro bought chairs with rough wood backs and seats woven from palm fronds to place on the hard sand floor of the front porch. The tables were made from wire spools discarded by a contractor that had installed a new power line along Highway 200. The spools were covered with oil cloth. A next door neighbor helped them build a brick cook stove and oven at one end of the porch. All the cooking area was open to view so that a diner could verify the hygienic attention paid to their meals.

Whereas street vendors only served tacos filled with mystery meats, Rusty wanted to make better use of Santa Rita's fishing industry. He tried different approaches and finally settled on a corn tortilla stuffed with a sautéed fish filet on a bed of shredded lettuce, cabbage and onions mixed with cream. The mixture was close to the recipe he remembered for his mother's coleslaw.

At first, only surfing friends came to eat fish tacos, but word-of-mouth advertising began to bring in some tourists. While Rusty staffed the cooking stove, Pedro welcomed customers and filled their drink orders by running to a nearby store for cold beer or Coca Cola. This way they avoided the cost of a liquor license. The idea of breaking the law was hardly a problem. Santa Rita seldom was patrolled by the county *Policia*.

The daily schedule at Casa de Cabra was as regular as the waves that rolled into Santa Rita Bay. Pedro rose early in the morning to clean up the previous night's detritus in the restaurant. Then he had a few hours to watch the surf and ride the best waves while Rusty prepared fish and vegetables for the lunch patrons. The responsibilities were set: Rusty worried about the food and Pedro worried about greeting diners, serving the tacos and cleaning up afterwards.

While Rusty and Pedro enjoyed the tranquility of Santa Rita, their brethren in the United States watched the hearings on Watergate. When Nixon resigned to avoid impeachment his departure left the country in the hands of Vice President Gerald Ford. Despite Ford's diplomacy, he could not overcome the growing pressure for a change in government and was defeated in the next election by Jimmy Carter. Carter's supporters were well rewarded when, as his first act in office, he "pardoned" all those who had left the country when faced with military service in Vietnam.

The presidential pardon ended the surfing and food serving days of the owners of Casa de Taco. The pardon allowed Rusty to return to Indiana. After a brief visit with his family he moved to Arizona and found a job selling real estate to Snowbirds who were trading northern winters for southern sun. Carter's actions allowed Pedro to return to his mother's hugging embraces and a grudging acceptance from Peter Senior. The price Pedro paid for his return was an immediate haircut and parental pressure to enroll in a community college business course. This was just enough to provide him the financial tools for an apprenticeship in the local office of Merrill Lynch.

Pedro, now back in the family fold as Peter, was surprised by the fact that his new job was actually interesting. Although he disliked spending much of his time in the computer-filled bullpen listening to the cacophony of all his peers talking on the phone at once, he was intrigued with the pace and the possibilities of his first real employment. He watched the more senior brokers operate and was fascinated that they seemed to be able to make large commissions with a minimum of mental or physical effort. The trick seemed to depend upon a large address book, lots of phone calls and the ability to sound like an expert on whatever stock Merrill Lynch was touting at the time. Pedro attached himself to a mentor that helped him learn how to read the tape and when to use the information to his advantage.

His days of handshake greetings to the taco-loving tourists and forced smiles made it easier for Peter to approach would-be investors. He excelled at selling the stocks that his employer held and needed to resell at a profit. Selling these stocks meant making good money, but it also meant experience in devising the strategy, negotiating a sale and the thrill of making a deal.

The commissions from increasing sales gave Peter a financial status that in turn improved his confidence amongst others. He began to shed his role as shy man on the fringes and move into a new one as man-about-town. He began accepting invitations to parties where his new outgoing manner placed him in contact with women that seemed interested in his thoughts and activities. When it came to female encounters, his experiences in Santa Rita had released him from his hesitancy. There he found that relationships were quickly established and easy to end without remorse with a continual parade of liberated women in and out of the village. Now back in California, he added a new air of bravado to his increasing skills as a party boy.

Peter continued his love affair with surfing and looked forward to meeting the few old friends that were still left hanging around Dogtown. They taught him better moves to stick with the curl of a wave and introduced him to new brands to get stoned with after they'd made a few good runs.

One of those trips to Dogtown further changed his life. After a long ride on a slow-breaking wave, he paddled back to the beach and came out of the white foam where it broke on shore. He headed for his Willys wagon. Watching other surfers coming back on shore, he recognized a woman with golden hair and a skin that glowed as the ocean water slowly drained away. He stopped and turned towards her.

"I know it's a lousy line, but don't I know you from somewhere?"

"It is a lousy line, but I think you were the first one to get me on a board. 'Name is Genie and we met at UCSB. Remember?"

"You haven't changed, except to get more beautiful."

This new Peter had learned that flattery might lead somewhere. He could now easily turn on a salesman's charm without first contemplating its consequences. In this case, his instinctive reaction could have been a mistake and he had to hold himself back. He had been attracted in Santa Barbara to this friendly Valley Girl, but she had rejected his approach. This time she seemed to be a little more ready to talk to him.

As they walked along the sand, Isabella Eugenia explained that she was from the town of Hemet near Riverside. Her mother was the daughter of a Mexican immigrant that had become a successful rancher. Her New Englander father was stationed briefly at the Fallon Navy Air Force Base in World War II and held a Yeoman's First Class rating. Her parents' immediate attraction to each other overcame wartime fears, and they were married in the St. Francis Chapel at the Mission Inn in Riverside. Her mother was eight months pregnant when an order for his overseas duty gave them just enough time for a few days to vacation across the border in Baja California. Perhaps it was her anxiety over his imminent departure that helped prompt a premature birth. Isabella Eugenia was born with dual American-Mexican citizenship.

After V-J Day, her father returned to California and went to work as a supervisor in a drug company warehouse. Because his pay only covered basic expenses for an expanding family, Genie supplemented the family income. She got a job as a temporary receptionist for a doctor's office as soon as she could pass for sixteen. She attended UCSB on a scholarship. While an undergraduate at Santa Barbara she fell in love with a six foot four Marine Lieutenant named Jorge Souza. Her friends joked that he must have been permanently posted outside her sorority house, given the amount of time he spent there. They were married in a chapel in La Jolla just before he went to Vietnam.

Peter found out later from other surfers that Genie was still struggling with the bad end to that youthful marriage. She didn't talk much about it, but Peter picked up from bit remarks that her former husband had been drafted, shipped to Vietnam and killed in a brothel brawl in Saigon. Her resulting bitterness was added to a sense of always being denied the fun and abstract attitude that money seemed to bring to women like her former, wealthier sorority sisters. A near depression at first made her seek solace on lonely beach walks, and then led her back into more serious surfing and the often experimental social life of Dogtown. There she could act the part of a sun worshipper but quietly cover her anxieties with alcohol, occasional Marijuana and an ever-present supply of uppers and downers.

Her lifestyle changed. One afternoon she noticed that another female surfer seemed to have a pattern of spending the day on the water but disappearing after the last run. She never seemed to participate in the partying. It was difficult not to talk shop with others and a loose bond developed between Genie and her new friend, Susan. One day Susan offhandedly suggested,

"Let's get out of here and look at the rest of Dogtown. I'm getting bored with the same old thing every day."

The two walked off the beach and passed by a building that probably was a well attended church when Venice was a national attraction. In front of its paint-frayed street entrance was a new aluminum and glass showcase announcing daily services inside the True Church of Christ The Savior. Susan placed a guiding hand on Genie's forearm and said,

"Oh, this might be a kick. Let's go in!"

A clean-shaven young man welcomed them. He was dressed in fading jeans topped by a grey shirt and white clerical collar.

"I am honored to have you enter our humble sanctuary. Please feel free to ask me questions or, if you prefer, simply enjoy this quiet release from the rapidly paced world outside."

The two women smiled at the man and moved towards one of the old wooden pews. Neither of them seemed to know what to do next. They finally sat down and, heads bowed, appeared lost in silent prayer until Susan turned to the cleric and said,

"It was nice to see you again, Reverend Bartholomew. I have enjoyed stopping in from time to time to listen to your sermons and would like you to meet my friend, Genie."

8

The visit to the True Church of Christ The Savior was repeated the following week. Genie was upset by the fading paint on the walls and scuffed up pews of the chapel but intrigued with the minister's lack of a forceful religious approach. He wasn't pressing any God talk upon her, but instead praised the joys of the sea and said how fortunate he was to be near the Pacific. Although she suspected that her friend might have a connection with the preacher, Genie was unaware that the two of them were slowly trying to convert her away from her Catholic heritage and Dogtown-supported lifestyle. The subterfuge became unimportant as each visit gave Genie an increasing sense of belonging to a sympathetic religious group. This in turn renewed her self-esteem.

Genie shook off her despair as she was introduced to the beliefs of the True Church of Christ The Savior. The evangelical fervor of members of the True Church provided Genie with a new positive attitude about her worth and a desire to reach out to the world. Every new person she met was greeted with a broad smile and soon softened by her apparent desire to share a love for life.

Her smiles and inclusiveness not only attracted Peter, but also soon snared him into a desire to live with this slim-waisted girl with shoulder-length hair highlighted by sun streaks. Peter's first hurdle for satisfying this desire was to join Genie on one of her visits to Reverend Bartholomew's Sunday service. Here Peter tried to keep his attention focused on the sermon by thinking of each new sentence as just another ocean wave with its troughs and crests to consider.

"We humans need DELIVERANCE from the GUILT of sin. We must be delivered from the PUNISHMENT due to the guilt of our sins. GOD can do this through divine SANCTIFICATION. In the words of the Apostle PAUL in Corinthians, 'But ye are washed, ye are SANCTIFIED'." He then gave an aside,

"Now all you surfers out there shouldn't be confused. Just because you guys are awash in salt water doesn't make you Baptized."

"Those whom God REGENERATES are given REPENTANCE, faith and inward renewal. Let us pray to be regenerated, to be BORN AGAIN!"

More church visits were a necessary part of the courtship. Peter soon lost interest in tying words to waves. Taking Bartholomew's preaching at face value, he tried to imagine being born again, if that's what he was supposed to do. The concept brought visions of a screaming mother-to-be and her blood-stained baby, the two still connected by the umbilical cord. He silently laughed as he compared the childbirth with surfing where a flexible safety cord binds the surfer and surfboard. The constant emphasis on SIN began to seriously worry him. What about all the pot? The screwing of those Indians out of their artifacts? The lies I tell to sell IPOs? Reverend Bartholomew had an answer.

"Every man since ADAM was born with a corrupt nature. They are spiritually DEAD. They can be brought back to life by accepting CHRIST as a savior. I say, 'Let JESUS into your heart!'

As Peter understood the situation, he had done a lot of sinful things, but they would be forgiven if his BEING was born again. To do that, he needed DELIV-ERANCE from the guilt of sin. He thought that he could get that if he said a Sinners Prayer and then sort of framed a picture in his mind of Jesus. Peter would be in charge of the process and could do it whenever he wanted to. Once he pictured the Jesus logo all his sins would be forgiven. He, Peter, could decide where and when it was to happen. He also liked the Reverend's further explanation.

"The Bible says, 'Salvation is the gift of God, not of works, lest any man should boast.'"

From that moment on Peter believed that his salvation was "*not of works.*" All the lies and cheating done on the job didn't count. For good measure, however, he swore off coffee, tea, beer and hard liquor to get God's forgiveness, but also in the hope that it would show up as a confirmation of his love for Genie. He was closer to asking her to marry him.

Genie's ultimate price for entrance to the marriage bed was that the wedding ser-vice be held in the True Church chapel. Genie and Susan had filled the altar area with bunches of gladiolas surrounded by green fern leaves to hide their mayon-naise jar containers. Redwood garlands were hung at the tops of each window.

The service was limited to respective families, her friend Susan, a few of the less scruffy surfing buddies and—out of the past—Successful realtor Rusty Rostovitz who drove over from Phoenix to act as Best Man. Prior to becoming *Isabella Eugenia Sessions, Isabella Eugenia Souza* spent time with Rusty learning about the exploits at Casa de Cabra. Rusty was happy to relive the days as he described them to Genie.

Rusty became softened by wedding euphoria and was further captured by Genie's winning smile. Peter sensed it as the right time to approach Rusty with a suggestion: the three of them should try to purchase the memorable Casa de Cabra as a jointly held vacation home. Peter's proposal was that each man would put up half the probable cost. Rusty wrote a check on the spot for $25,000.00 US. Peter also wrote a similar check and put them both in his pocket.

After the wedding Peter and Genie flew to Mexico to purchase Casa de Cabra. At the time such an act was patently illegal because the Mexican government prohibited foreigners from owning land within 50 kilometers of the ocean. Peter, however, learned that there was a sneaky way around the complex land laws in the *Ejito* community of Santa Rita. The Mexican government did allow some of the commonly owned land in the village to be parceled out and sold to individual Mexicans. Armed with this knowledge, Peter arranged a meeting with the Ejito Council so that Genie could request purchase of the land around Casa de Cabra. Happy to receive the income, the council sold the property to Isabella Eugenia Sessions. It was not mere coincidence that Peter married a girl with dual Mexican-American citizenship.

Peter failed to tell Rusty that the purchase price for Casa de Cabra was actually only $25,000. Rusty's check paid for the property and Peter's check was torn up. Through Genie's dual citizenship, Peter effectively owned the place. The shell game wasn't apparent to Rusty. The local records of the transaction, such as they were, were written in Spanish legalese and he never wasted the time to review them on his few visits to Santa Rita. Rusty had more pressing concerns with the southwest real estate markets that were fast diminishing as high interest rates made mortgage loans prohibitive. This threatened to close down the Scottsdale subdivision that had created his life savings.

Genie and Peter had a greater problem of their own. It surfaced at a time when the Reagan administration was wrapped up in the Iran-Contra investigations.

Then, during his seventh year in office, while Reagan made history in Berlin by urging Soviet leader Gorbachev to "tear down this wall," his country's stock market was hit with the largest one day percentage drop in history.

This plunge affected the young Sessions because Peter had become a student and disciple of creative brokering. The simple act of selling stocks to prospective clients that were enchanted with the myth of an ever-present bull market wasn't challenging enough for Peter. He graduated into IPOs, Initial Public Offerings, of upstart companies that were made impressive by marketing hype but would not last a year. From IPOs he moved to mutual funds and eagerly filled a risky role as an insider trader, selling or buying funds for his clients after the markets had closed. He loved the work. It was all like making a dirty tennis shot.

This time it wasn't like a tennis match where he could just walk off the court. Peter learned from an insider trading partner that the New York Stock Exchange computers had just suffered from their worst-ever breakdown due to an investor anxiety attack. The entire system became completely useless when mutual fund managers all tried to sell their various holdings at the same time. Peter was scared that the debacle would open up an investigation about trading mutual funds. This meant that Peter's job, their home, their capital, everything was threatened; but much worse was the contemplation of a possible lawsuit and jail sentence.

He rushed home, briefly explained his fears to Genie and the two packed all their belongings. After a brief stop at the Wells Fargo branch to withdraw all their ready funds, they headed south. Their Jeep Cherokee traveled almost the same route to Mexico that Peter's Willys took when he went there to dodge the draft. Now they were making a similar escape.

The two spent their first months back in Santa Rita camping out in Casa de Cabra where they could look down at the masses of palm trees that defined the break between beach sand and green foliage. They were enjoying the great surfing again, but Genie knew that they were slowly eating away their dollars. One day, with that constant smile disguising her real concern, Genie suggested a plan.

"There are empty parking garages down below that must have been built when the first owners thought they were going to occupy the Casa. If we could talk our parents into lending us the money, we could turn the garages into rental rooms.

There's no good hotel in town and more and more tourists want a place to stay here."

"Let's make the parents partners! I'll worry about the construction and you can take care of the operations."

Genie saw this only as an escape from this camping-out phase of their marriage, but Peter quickly bought into the idea of being an innkeeper. He liked having partners that bore all the money risks. He liked being back in Santa Rita. Peter was once again Pedro.

It was easy to find willing helpers. Pedro hired one named Manuel who soon became a combined *Jefe* and *Architecto*. Although Pedro imagined that, in thinking up ideas for the remodeling, he had discovered his own latent design abilities; this was only because Manuel was smart enough to make him think so. To prepare for renters, the old garage walls were strengthened and doors and windows placed on the ocean side of the new rooms. Although the rooms opened to a community road right outside, Pedro figured that the water views far outweighed any nuisances from passersby. Because only minimal daylight was coming from the oceanside, the rear walls of the old garages were removed to open the ends of the rooms to the sky. The resulting walls were bare stone where laborers digging away at the hillside had exposed the rock formation.

While Pedro escaped to his surfboard to worry about bathroom plans for each of the three units, Manuel got a friend to install showers on the rock walls. Water was supplied to the showers through pieces of hollow bamboo that emptied into a coconut shell that had been pierced to provide a shower spray. Washbasins were formed out of smooth stones and mortar. The washbasin fittings were the cast pineapples, lizards, and turtles that normally were sold as ornamental garden faucets.

The details were left to Manuel. Some problems, such as stopping the flooding when heavy summer rains came through the opening or eliminating the stench of the waste water dumped into the nearby ocean, were simply forgotten. Pedro had a motto that overrode even his newly-found forgiveness of past sins by the True Church of Jesus Christ.

"Never look back in the car mirror. In the time it takes to see who's behind you, they've already crashed your rear end."

9

MAY 13, 1988

Pedro and Genie Sessions drove from Santa Rita to Mazatlan in order to shop at the new *Gigante* market. In the parking lot, Genie stepped down from their Jeep Cherokee and walked between parked cars along the cobblestone path that led to the store. Pedro got out, locked the doors and followed her. Inside the automatic glass doors, Genie grabbed a push cart and headed for the dairy section. Pedro passed by the hardware and house wares aisles and noticed that the racks were barely filled when compared with those in the more familiar Safeway in Santa Monica. Overhead lights directed their brightest rays to the more expensive goods on the top shelves.

Walking into the next section, however, he found that fruits and vegetables were piled high. There were ample supplies of produce from local growers. Standing beside a counter loaded chest high with egg cartons, he noticed one with a dried yolk streak. Something connected the carton and its simple flaw with all that had happened to him in the last decade. He compared the moments of success to the perfectly shaped, unbroken eggs in their paper-mâché nests. He liked the vision of his accomplishments all nicely ordered within an overall framework. Was the framework that omnipresent salvation described by Genie's pastor? Yes! He was finding his place in the world. His driving ambition to be great could be achieved through a series of individual financial gains. If there was ever a taint to his money goals, he was sure his absolution would come from embracing Jesus. God would take care of the dirty yellow stains.

Genie pushed the cart with her purchases towards the checkout counter. She paused to watch Pedro in the Men's section fingering a short sleeved shirt. She wondered how they had gotten to this point where Pedro seemed to have fallen back into a lifestyle familiar to him but one new, and possibly threatening, to her. Was this God's Way? Would he soon again provide the light that shone so brightly for her in the True Church of Christ? Alternatively, was this God's Will, tying her into an irreversible relationship with an unfamiliar world? Was there a problem with the place......or with the man?

Pedro had been busy since returning from Mazatlan. He was in one of the new bedrooms in the converted garage. He was in the middle of a long and unpleasant cleanup of the shower area with water, detergent and chlorine. He wasn't sure about the reason for the mess, but he knew it had to be cleaned before anyone else saw it. The room reeked from the mixture and he only wanted to escape into the surf where the odors and memory of what he had just done might disappear. He had seen a few injuries from surfing, but the sight of so much blood was new to him. Red splotches still covered much of the rock shower wall and broken images of his faded Luau shirt were reflected in a scarlet puddle near the floor drain.

Pedro didn't want anyone to point accusing fingers towards the hotel or even towards him. He was sure the blood had come from the room's occupant or someone that had access to it. If this meant there'd been some kind of criminal act, there would be some kind of investigation. In his favor, the Mexican law enforcement was casual, particularly when it involved foreigners. There needed to be some way to head off inquiries, to give the authorities a quick answer so that the event would be soon forgotten. This might have been an attack, but it could also have been a suicide. He looked for some kind of explanation. There was no letter, no weapon and no message scrawled in blood on the floor or in lipstick on the mirror. He spoke to the wall.

"There's no evidence. Everyone is suspect. I've got to do something."

He then wrote a note on a pad he found beside the bed. At the top of the notepad were the words *Casa de Mastil*. Genie had suggested the name *Casa de Mastil* for their new venture. *Mastil* was a Spanish word for the mast of a ship. Pedro liked the implication of a strong thrust, braving all that confronted it. To promote the concept, Manuel had set the mast from of an old wooden sailboat into a concrete base near the road. A sketch of the mast became the official logo for the would-be hotel. It was printed on all their stationary.

Pedro contemplated his next move. He talked to the room.

"I've acted too fast. This is blood from Genie's friend, or at least from someone the friend let into the bedroom. I've been too quick to try to cover for us......for Genie. Genie! Why did she have to ask this one down here? That note might not be a good idea."

As he turned to retrieve the single sheet of paper his eye caught an unusual view through the bedroom window. He saw that a crowd had formed on the beach around one of the fishing skiffs. This wasn't just a welcome home for the fishermen. This was a group of curious people, slowly shaking their heads and backing away from the boat. If this had something to do with the blood he'd tried to remove, Pedro knew that he had to be in that crowd and identified with its concern in case anyone got suspicious about his role in the mystery. He knew that he had to be seen as sharing their interest, but he guessed that walking directly to the crowd might establish a too-quick connection to the fledgling hotel. Perhaps, with the right action, he could keep his Casa de Mastil out of the picture. Forgetting the note, he decided to paddle around the point with his board and then, after a reasonable time, head back to the main beach. No one would remember where he'd come from or how long he'd been there.

Pedro removed his board from a storage closet near the end of the old garage and started towards *La Playa de los Muertos*, so named because the Beach of the Dead adjoined the local cemetery. He was not comfortable with the implications of this route that took him by the scattered graves, some marked by concrete crosses, some by headstones with names, but most just by slabs of concrete covering the grave. Although it had been months since celebrating the Day of the Dead, some of the gravestones held remnants of wilting flowers. Others were draped with dusty, plastic-wrapped wreaths of artificial roses and hibiscus. Pedro walked uphill by all this and passed a new concrete block mausoleum on his right as he went downhill. The mausoleum was covered with ceramic roof tiles but its openings were secured by the kind of rough grille work used on factory gates. Santa Ritans had to make do with what was locally available.

He felt better as he eased his board into the breaking surf and began the trip around the rocky point. Rather than following the shoreline as it curved back to the town beach, Pedro headed to a point well out from the crowd that was still gathered around the boat. He watched the roll of the waves, taking the best ones for a short distance and then returning to the takeoff spot in order to pass the delay time he thought appropriate. Finally, he caught one high enough to carry him close to the beach. Correctly acting his part, he walked ashore with his board under his right arm and headed to the crowd. He heard someone ask,

"Who is she?" Her gender was obvious from glimpses of the naked body that lay in the gunwales of the fishing boat. Two men arrived with a blanket to cover the body. An older woman clutched the crucifix hanging from her neck on a gold chain and slowly chanted, "*Dios santo, Dios santo...salvarnos, salvarnos.*"

The local dog pack had sensed the excitement and lingered near the boat hoping that this gathering, which to them looked like a large family beach picnic, might produce a scrap of food. One of the men reached towards a portly matron with a young baby in her arms. He urged her to go and call the Policia. Truthfully, he didn't want their child, however young and unaware, to be tainted by the horrible sight.

"We have to find out who she is....or was." The words were from one of the Gringo surfers.

"Here comes Pedro. Maybe he knows."

"Anyone missing from your new hotel, Pedro?"

"What's going....what's the crowd....Oh My God in Heaven, what a horrible thing to see." mouthed the surprised looking newcomer. "My hotel? No, no one. Of course we haven't officially opened, so there are no guests registered with us. Perhaps she fell off a boat?" He watched while the blanket was hoisted up and over the body. He could see that the head had been battered and the arms severely slashed below the shoulders.

The pale white body was all that was left of Susan Brent Warner, Genie's friend from Dogtown and the True Church. Susan was the daughter of the very successful founder and owner of Socal Savings and Loan in Stockton, California. She was a product of her time, growing up with new wealth and attending the Catholic All Saints Academy. Susan wanted liberation from the stricture of nuns and the social limitations of Stockton. She enrolled at the new Santa Cruz campus of the University of California. There she found a lifestyle amongst students that were similarly freed and nurtured by a laid-back faculty. Unfortunately for Susan, the liberation was too complete. She began to question her family's way of life and was quick to support any new reactive cause. Ultimately she began to experiment with marijuana and made a jump to LSD and other life-threatening drugs. Flunking out of college, she spent a decade in rehab and halfway houses until she believed that she'd found the right direction with the True church of Christ Our Savior.

Genie had invited Susan to spend a few days at Casa de Mastil to help with the opening. Genie knew that Pedro would appreciate the added free labor. Now she wondered where her friend was. She had gone looking for her and found only an empty room. It held an antiseptic aroma like she'd smelled in the hallways of the local clinic. She confronted Pedro when he returned from his mingling with the crowd on the beach:

"Where is Susan? What's that smell in her room? What's the crowd for on the beach?"

"I don't know how to tell you this. It's all horrible."

Pedro, still wet and carrying his board, felt a burden far worse than his Jeff Ho Zephyr. Genie looked at her husband as if he were a complete stranger. Shock, question, and hatred all showed at once.

"What have you done to Susan?"

"I didn't do it. I didn't touch her. This will ruin us. Why? Why now, just as we open?"

"What do you mean? What are you talking about?"

"She's gone, Genie. Her body's out there in that boat on the beach. I saw her. There was blood all over her room. I had to clean it up. I had to clean it up. That's our best unit."

Now in tears at the knowledge unfolding before her, Genie muttered through clenched teeth,

"I've lost one of my best friends and all you can worry about is what it will do to this damned hostel!" Her last word was carefully picked. This was a chance to unleash the enmity built up over differing views about details. She wanted the best, he wanted the cheapest.

"Where's Emilio? Perhaps he knows something. I'm going down to the beach." Genie walked away. It was the first time that Pedro had ever seen her without the smile.

Emilio? Where to find him? Emilio was the first official onsite employee of Casa de Mastil, hired as a gopher and possibly a potential desk clerk. They knew little more about him than that he was one of Manuel's many cousins. In a town like Santa Rita, isolated for centuries, everyone was probably someone's cousin with varying degrees of removal. Emilio was hired because he looked strong enough to carry guest luggage and could help build a set of steps from the Casa de Cabra to the new units on the road down below.

Emilio was not to be seen anywhere at Casa de Mastil. Pedro walked the half mile to Manuel's, hoping to find him there.

10

The crowd around the boat began to disburse when a police vehicle arrived at the beach. Few Santa Ritans cared to become involved with the authorities. The police car carried Detective Sergeant Jaime Gonzalez and a junior officer. They stepped out of the car accompanied by the local pharmacist who was the closest thing Santa Rita had to a coroner. They all looked at the body. Hoping to sound knowledgeable but quite unsure of his diagnosis, the would-be *Juez* pronounced:

"The woman has been dead for between one and three days."

The three officials realized that the ocean had wiped out any immediate clues and agreed that the victim should be carried by the junior officer to the *deposito de cadaveres* in Culiacan for an autopsy. A doctor there could examine teeth and possibly determine the cause of death.

On the beach Sergeant Gonzalez got a quick answer of NO every time he asked if anyone knew or knew of the victim. The sergeant figured that, given the light skin color, it was probable that the body belonged to a foreigner. He turned to one of the few remaining onlookers and asked,

"Who in town is taking in tourists?"

The list was short. After getting directions, he made his first stop at La Barracca, the oldest and most authentically Spanish building in town. Given the early part of the season, only one guest had signed the register during the week. He was from Mexico and sitting now on the front porch. When told of the circumstances, the B&B owner suggested that the sergeant might stop at two other houses across the Plaza, and then vaguely mentioned that those new Gringos out near the point might have guests.

When the Sergeant found that there had been no guests at the houses on the Plaza, he followed directions that led to Casa de Cabra. He stopped at what looked to be a newly-made entrance to the casa. He noticed the young palm trees that lined the driveway, aspiring to become the markers of a grand entrance. The drive ended at a turnaround circle partially paved with rings of brick, tile and river-washed stone. Beyond the circle was a round palapa with an open porch that circled the entire perimeter. Finding no one in immediate view and seeing no entry door, he climbed the few stairs to the porch and followed it to the ocean side of the casa. Santa Rita Bay and an endless Pacific Ocean came into view. Gonzalez was immediately drawn towards the panoramic beauty. He stopped short of the edge when he saw that there was no guard rail to protect anyone from what looked like a ten meter drop.

A lone figure sat on the porch floor near its edge, her arms clasped over raised knees. Sun-bleached hair fell over her legs as she pressed her head against her arms and knees. Gonzalez figured she might be briefly resting her eyes from the ocean's glare but could also be grappling with a troubling thought.

"*Con permisso, Señorita. Soy Sargento Jaime Alvaro González Diaz.*" The sergeant enjoyed announcing his position.

Genie immediately switched on her smile. "*Por favor, Señora Isabela Eugenia Sessions, Sargento.*" The relationship was established and her status understood.

Gonzalez presented his credentials and excused himself again for bothering Senora Sessions. While he explained why he was there, Genie smiled, only changing to acknowledge the sympathy or shock expected when Gonzalez presented some of the more lurid aspects of the case.

"By chance, did the Sessions have guests during the week, particularly a female visitor?" he asked. Genie was quick to describe her visiting friend Susan and verify that she had not been seen that day.

"Perhaps she took the bus that stopped in Santa Rita on its route from Culiacan." She described Susan as a very independent woman who left them often for long walks on the beach. Assuming that the interview had ended, Genie got up to escort the Sergeant back to the road. Gonzalez thanked her for her time, and then asked if, unofficially, he might look around the new Casa de Mastil. He excused the request as a reason to learn more about such a great addition to Santa Rita. Genie showed him their half-completed casa.

Gonzalez asked if he could see the new units on his way back to town. After going down the one hundred and fifty new brick steps that Emilio had installed, the two stopped before the renovated old garage. Genie opened the door to the first unit and urged Gonzalez to look it over, hoping that this would assuage any curiosity to look further. Gonzalez remarked about the novelty of the bathroom and admired the interior colors. Genie hesitated to offer more of the tour, but knew that he might insist and doubted that local laws required such a thing as a search warrant.

It had been five years since the adoption of Article 9 of the Mexican Constitution. This in effect repealed any idea that Mexico was run by the Napoleonic code that deemed everyone guilty until proven innocent. The new article didn't guarantee that the concept had trickled down to the State of Sinaloa police. When she finally asked the question, he said that of course he would like to see the other units. The minute that Sergeant Gonzalez opened the glass door to the middle unit, he caught the smell of chlorine that still clung in the air from Pedro's cleanup. He walked into the room and traced the odor to the exposed rock wall and tiled shower floor. A large area of the wall was still damp.

"Senora Sessions. What is the strange smell?" He asked, knowing that the odor was too strong for her to deny its existence.

"I am not sure. Perhaps my husband or our helper Emilio was cleaning spilled paint or…that's it….removing the mould that forms on the rock wall."

"Senora, is this the room where your friend Miss Susan stays?" he asked and then continued, "Is this possibly a message from her?" Gonzalez picked up a small piece of note paper and handed it to her.

Genie looked at the note and was about to read it to the Sergeant until she saw its short message.

"My life has been a constant wreck. Please forgive me for what I am going to do. You have been my only true friend, Genie. I love you. Susan."

Genie recognized the handwriting. She returned it to Gonzalez, saying, "The note is to me. It is about my friendship with Susan."

Pedro had crossed town to find Manuel who was spraying down the dust on the dirt road in front of his house. Behind Manuel, Pedro could see a square block façade covered with a rust-colored paint. Openings in the wall were without glass but protected with wrought iron grilles. There was no front yard to separate the house from whatever happened on the street.

"Hola, Manuel, es Emilio aquí?"

"No, Senor Pedro."

Like most conversations with Manuel, his statement was brief. Seeking elaboration, Pedro told him about the crowd gathered on the beach and announced that Genie's friend was missing. He added that her body might be what the crowd was looking at in the boat. He slowly worked up to the question but finally asked point blank if Emilio was a responsible person. Manuel made a guarded reply.

"He is *serio* now, after being away so long."

Manuel was pushed until he eventually said that "being away so long" meant being up north in Chihuahua. Being in Chihuahua meant being in prison. Being in prison meant a long stay in a maximum security jail. A maximum security jail was for rapists and murderers. Emilio had been accused of raping and then terminating the life of a high school girl. A lack of witnesses convinced the judges—Mexican courts have no juries—that the incarceration should be limited to ten years. Now, according to Manuel, Emilio was out of *prisión* and a responsible person.

Pedro slowly walked to Casa de Cabra pondering the best way to face Genie. He found her alone, waiting on the driveway when he returned. Sergeant Gonzalez had left, advising that they not leave town without permission from the authorities. Pedro took a breath and said,

"I can't believe this is happening to me! Susan is not here. Emilio is not here. There is a crowd looking at a mutilated body on the beach. Manuel finally admitted that Emilio has a murderer's record!"

"You might first consider that it is also happening to me, that Susan was my best friend and that you were the one that hired Emilio."

"Do you think they might suspect that one of us did it? My God, My God! We need a lawyer."

"I would think the first thing is to call Susan's father."

"What can I tell him? He'll think that I'm responsible."

"Are you?"

Sergeant Gonzalez spent the next day in Culiacan, presenting his view of the dilemma of the unidentified female body to the Public Prosecutor. Gonzalez described how the body had been found by fishermen. He reported his assumption that the body belonged to a guest from Casa de Mastil and his suspicions about the roles of Eugenia and Peter Sessions. The Public Prosecutor, after confirming from the dental work that the victim was undoubtedly a *Norte Americano,* called upon the Judicial Police to investigate the circumstances surrounding the death. Their findings in Santa Rita concluded that there had been a serious blood bath and subsequent attempt at a cleanup in the room at Casa de Mastil.

When the police asked about the suicide note, Pedro admitted that he had hastily cleaned up the room in order to save the reputation of the fledgling hotel. He said that he had written the note to give an immediate answer for the cause of death. It was meant to put the blame on the unfortunate suicide victim, and avoid possible accusations that his hotel was at fault. When it looked like they might consider him a prime suspect, Pedro related his discussion with Manuel.

A police officer was dispatched to learn more about the cousin from Manuel and finally a call was sent out to apprehend and detain Emilio. He was found working as a laborer cultivating Agave plants on a farm near Tequila and taken to Mazatlan in handcuffs. There, the Public Prosecutor presented his case to a judge of the criminal court and Emilio was convicted and sent back to Chihuahua.

Although Pedro breathed a brief sigh of relief, he soon had to answer to Susan's father, Brent Warner, who had the advantage of being represented by the attorneys of Socal Savings and Loan. Warner accused Pedro of complicity, forgery, knowingly hiring a criminal and failing to properly protect hotel guests. A lawsuit was filed in Santa Monica, Pedro's legal residence. To avoid further publicity,

Peter Sessions Senior pleaded with Warner to settle the case out of court for an undisclosed amount. Silence cost him his small fortune.

11

Enid and Doug Williams were headed for Santa Rita. Their property in San Miguel Allende had been sold and they were investigating coastal towns along the Pacific. They toured south to Manzanillo and the Colima coast. They viewed beachfront properties that were too exposed to crashing waves and visited towns that looked to be 5 years away from having a store or restaurant. Doug began to see the trip as just another example of Enid's restlessness. She always seemed to want to be somewhere else. Before he had the chance to complain, Enid suggested that they head north and re-visit the village where they had spent vacation days before buying in San Miguel.

They turned off Highway 200 and drove into Santa Rita. They first stopped at *La Castillo*. Despite the implication of the name, the B&B had only a few rooms and none were available. The helpful manager suggested that a new hotel called Casa de Mastil might have space. They followed his directions to a rutted route along the ocean front until they found a portal covered with brilliant maroon Bougainvillea. Inside the entrance they could see a short, well-tanned man dressed in jams and a faded Luau shirt. His blonde hair reached to his shirt collar. His welcoming wave of a hand suggested a willingness to help.

Doug stopped the car and asked him if he knew whether the hotel had any open rooms. The man leaned into the car window, shook hands with each of the Williams and explained that he, "Call me Pedro," was the proprietor of the establishment. He thought that he might have a possible free space and asked them if they'd like a tour of Casa de Mastil and a look at his available inventory. Enid wasn't sure about the man. His smile seemed artificial, turned on like a cat facing a meal of mice, and his handshake was almost limp and, yes, slippery. It seemed that he really didn't like touching others, as if they might be transmitting a fatal disease. She mentioned this to Doug as they started the tour; but Doug said that he had had enough driving and was eager to stop for the night.

The Williams soon were relaxing in new wicker lounge chairs on the balcony of a suite that Pedro had just finished building over the original three-bedroom structure. Near its entry door a ceramic sign with a border of hand-painted flowers announced that the suite was called *Villa Romantico*. With a slightly shaking hand, Doug brought out a leather-covered glass flask and poured a quarter of its contents into a ceramic cup. Like the entry sign, the cup was decorated with a pattern of brilliant and varied blossoms. Enid winced and shook her head when Doug asked her to join him. She saw the flask as an affectation, Doug's memo of the good old days at UVA, the University of Virginia. The wince was reflexive, a calculated response to watching alcohol slowly attack Doug from one side while the increasing effects of Parkinson's gnawed at him from the other.

Enid was actually a contraction of her given name, Enide. Her parents were innocently clairvoyant about her future when they named her after a Celtic heroine that was constantly abused by her husband, Eric. They could not have foreseen Enid's constant physical problems; or how they would have affected her future. Enid suffered from severe back pain. Her troubles began while she was still enrolled at Smith College. She and three fellow students were spending their summer vacation touring France. The driver of the day had spent his senior year commuting between Amherst and Smith. The previous evening he'd asked Enid to marry him. He never lived to carry out his proposal. On the next day their Citroen Deux Chevaux engine failed at a remote railroad crossing. The approaching train engineer saw them and instantly blew a warning siren but simply could not stop in time. Three in the car died instantly.

Enid, the sole survivor, was to be forever plagued by spinal pain that she'd cover up with a forced enthusiasm for trying something new: a new dress, a new cause, a new place to visit. This spirit made it easier for her to consider a proposal from her dead fiancée's brother, even though it was not long after the accident. He did this out of what he thought was a sense of duty, fulfilling a filial obligation to his dead sibling. The marriage resulted in the birth of two children, but was a mismatch from the start. There was little reason for Enid to continue the charade. She divorced him to marry an older man who soon died of a heart attack.

Douglas Williams brought a similarly mixed history to the marriage. The only son of a New York couple, Doug was brought up to survive in the country club atmosphere of Long Island. At their death, he had no trouble spending the trust income from his parent's estate. He enjoyed the parties and could pace his drinking by telling amusing tales about the days at UVA or repeating stockbroker jokes heard at his office. His first wife was just the opposite and covered her anxieties by over-consumption in the alcohol and canapé laden social life that came naturally to Doug. She lost herself to Manhattans and Gin Fizzes and continued her heavy drinking through her first pregnancy. Her drinking didn't stop after the birth of their daughter and finally led to divorce. Doug took a second chance on his future and married his secretary, Victoria. She bore him a son; but the differing cultures never merged. Doug, like Enid, now had two former spouses; but unlike Enid, who had alimony from her first husband and inherited funds from her second, Doug had the unpleasant baggage from two expensive divorces.

A dejected Doug moved to Steamboat Springs in the northern Colorado Rockies where he hoped to renew a life of skiing that had started before WWII. His parents often took him to Davos, the Swiss town that was known then by socialites as the "best" of the winter resorts. There he learned to ski and his experience made him an excellent candidate for the 10th Mountain Division. He saw duty in both Colorado and Italy. Doug was happy with his choice of Steamboat where he could balance his evening partying against the daytime physical challenges of a mountain life. He met Enid at a UVA reunion party in Denver. After a summer spent commuting between the Western Slope and the Front Range, they were married. She joined him in Steamboat happy to see a new group of faces, new scenery and the prospects of a romantic life in a new log home. After five years of cold mountain weather and with Doug showing signs of an increasing infirmity, Enid insisted that they needed a warm climate as a winter refuge.

The next morning Pedro suggested they join him for breakfast at *Mango-Mango* in town. Pedro told them about his early surfing days and his discovery of Santa Rita. After giving an embroidered explanation of how he and Genie had been attracted to the area, he approached the question,

"Would you be interested in buying property here?"

"Why, we might be." Enid replied.

"I am building three new villas on the hill east of the village. Would you like to see them?"

"I guess it won't hurt to, but we would want to be close to the beach," was Doug's immediate answer.

Doug looked to Enid for some sign of agreement, hoping that she would support his desire to avoid steep roads and difficult to traverse pathways. Even though science was yielding new information about and medications to ease the effects of Parkinson's, Doug knew there still was no cure for the disease. The nerve cells in his brain were simply not producing enough of the vital chemical Dopamine to insure smooth coordination of his muscles. He was beginning to see a slight, constant and uncontrollable tremor of each hand. His doctors had warned him that this would be the start of increasing debilitation that would slow his walking and impair his balance.

For a man who enjoyed the companionship of others and was devoted to outdoor exercise, his only option was to adapt to a future of halting words and a stuttering shuffle. This meant an increasing dependence upon Enid for assistance and financial support as medical bills began to eat away the estate inherited from his parents. Enid's constant reference to her back problems didn't help. Doug confided with friends,

"I've never known anyone that could have so many different ailments from the same back injury,"

Pedro drove them across the bridge and followed a diagonal road along the town soccer field. They passed three horses browsing and a lone cow tethered in the vegetation beside the road. As Pedro headed up a very steep, cobble-stoned street, Doug observed,

"We could never do this in the snow at home,". Pedro slowed at the crest and then braked to stop at what Doug guessed was the first of the newly constructed residences. He was surprised by the shape of the structure. There was not one straight wall.

Enid and Doug followed Pedro down a steep flight of steps to a large, flat stone that was an entry stoop to what appeared to be a general living space. The space was defined by curving walls that separated it from bedrooms on either side. The walls supported a palapa made from wood beams and woven palm fronds. The concrete floor extended out to an unfenced edge that seemed to be in flight over the hilltop. Enid and Doug were surprised by the strange architecture. They couldn't conceal their bewilderment and really didn't know what to say. Pedro saw the look and quickly said,

"Now, you might not like this, but I wanted you to see my work in process."

"We would like to be closer to the water," Enid responded. "My husband is not well, and the long walk from here to the beach would be impossible for him."

The day was spent with Pedro driving along the dusty roads of Santa Rita. They viewed property on the beach that looked subject to erosion from summer storms. They drove into the jungle on the fringes of town and looked at too-remote sites that were high above a rocky coastline. They looked at row houses in the center of a town that needed, but missed, the urbanizing style brought there by Spanish conquerors. Pedro continued his soft sales pitch, hoping not to sound too eager to make a sale.

"Would you be interested in being part of Casa de Mastil? Perhaps we could find you a proper spot?" He drove them back to Casa de Mastil and pointed out a bench of land.

"This could be yours and you would have the benefits of our *boutique*—he liked the word—hotel services. We have a marketing program if you are interested in renting your villa when you are not here." He waited.

"I can build you something like what you saw up the hill, with much better materials of course." He waited again.

"Two bedrooms would cost Two Hundred Fifty."

"Pesos or Dollars?" Doug innocently asked, still unable to quickly calculate the equivalents or put Mexican prices into focus versus those across the border.

Pedro interpreted the question as a joke and went on to say, "Because you would be part of the hotel, you could rent out the villa when you are not here."

"We will think about it seriously," said Enid.

Enid's serious thinking time was reduced to only a few minutes of talk between the Williams. Enid distrusted Pedro and disliked what she'd seen of his design work, but she was attracted to his proposition and explained why to her husband.

"This is good. We have a direct flight from Denver to Mazatlan. We have a man that will build us a villa. Because it's part of his hotel, it will be well built. We can be close to the beach, get rents and have someone to watch our place when we are not here. I'm ready to sign up."

"What are you signing? How can we own a place here when the Mexicans don't allow foreign ownership near the ocean? How do we know this guy is honest? What do we get for two hundred fifty K?"

"It's my money, Dear."

12

Enid and Doug Williams returned from Santa Rita to a bright October day in Steamboat Springs. In contrast to the lush Mexican foliage, Colorado's summer green had turned brown. Aspens had been stripped bare in one night by a western wind that left them exposed. There was now a veiled transparency where once there'd been masses of gold. Enid hated these gray days and looked forward to Christmastime when a protective blanket of winter snow would cover the temporary blemishes. To counter the Autumnal blues, Enid joined the other local neo-natives that filled these days with rehearsals for mini-musicals or mystery plays. They were assured of at least three performances before the Christmas week crowds lost interest. These new but now entrenched citizens had come to Steamboat for the winter skiing and summer fishing. They also were attracted by the history of the old town that was missing in the newer resorts like Vail or Beaver Creek down highway 131. Walking along the main street, they passed by many old brick buildings with their original windows and doors now preserved as professional offices or boutique shops. The name of Steamboat Springs went back to the days when Pioneers on their way west stopped to get fresh water near a rocky promontory on the Yampa River. There the rush of the river past the rock created a whistle that reminded them of the boats they had left behind on the Missouri or the Mississippi.

Their possible purchase in Casa de Mastil was never discussed by the Williams. Enid simply announced one day that she wanted to go ahead with purchasing her own villa and called Pedro to ask for more details about the purchase and ownership. He answered some of her questions, and followed up with a fax copy of an agreement form. He assured her that it contained all the information she needed; but Enid couldn't forget the distrust generated in their first meeting.

Despite having excluded him from the decision, she showed the agreement to Doug. She needed another opinion and Doug was available, even though she wasn't thrilled with his business history. He had jumped from commercial banking to selling stocks to selling electrical switch gear throughout the Midwest. When he retired, he invested in a credit card scheme that offered discounts to a card holder for shopping at approved hardware stores. The idea came from Ted Starman who needed Doug for the financing. Starman was a familiar name in the Williams' household. Ted and Mary Starman were always present at any of Enid's parties. They created special dishes for the guests based on recipes from their operation of a now-defunct gourmet cooking school. Enid and Doug readily accepted that their new "best of friends" were victims of fraudulent bookkeeping at the school. Mary didn't explain that she was the bookkeeper.

In addition to the Doug-Ted partnership, Mary and Enid had jointly opened a new jewelry store in Steamboat. Mary would provide the sales expertise and Enid the money to get started. Profits would be equally shared. While the Williams were in Santa Rita, Mary Starman secured a lease in a new strip shopping mall that was designed to echo the old brick architecture of the main street. She carried the old-west theme into the shop and filled it with the work of local artisans and Southwest Indians. The store income would depend upon Mary's skill in selling, particularly to second homeowners.

Doug was looking at the four-page agreement that Pedro had sent Enid.

"The damned thing doesn't even have paragraphs. How can we refer to things we may want to change?"

The agreement briefly stated that Peter and Isabella Eugenia Sessions would construct a 2-bedroom villa with living space and kitchen to be located "on the grounds of Casa de Mastil." It called for an up-front payment of 50% and 12 equal monthly payments of the balance. The agreement gave the purchasers the right to occupy the villa for no more than 90 days per year so that at other times Pedro could rent the unit to tourists.

The purchasers would pay $285.00 per month for maintenance and light housekeeping services and Pedro would take 25% of the rentals as commission. A separate paragraph noted that Isabella Eugenia, with her dual citizenship, would be the *Presta Nombre* for the property. The Spanish name was new to the Williams. This would take some research.

Doug took the papers to his office, a small space rented on the top floor of the former Odd Fellows Hall. He liked the carved marble plaque announcing IOOF that still was mortared into the brick street-side wall. There he wanted to re-type

the material on a Compaq LTE computer that he had purchased for his enter-
prises. Happily, the Parkinson's hadn't begun to limit his finger action. Understanding Pedro's terminology was not easy and the challenge of using the Word
Perfect software slowed down his output. His first task was to reorganize the top-
ics into separate divisions with their own numbers and subject descriptions. A
major item was missing. In the first paragraph he added the phrase,

"The Sessions hereby agree to sell all rights to land as described herein and construct a villa as described below."

Wanting a more detailed description of the villa, he called Pedro to request a set
of plans. A week later he received a one-page fax with a sketch that roughly out-
lined the spaces: three circles to indicate kitchen and bedrooms sat outside a central area labeled *La Sala*. There were no defined bathrooms or closets. Numerous
side calculations had converted square meters to 1800 square feet.

Doug thought that a proper document should define three different types of control to be effective: cost, area and quality. Given the area and cost descriptions, he
needed to fix the quality level. From the start, Genie Sessions had insisted that
each hotel unit have its own cute name. The first three in the old garage were
called *Tranquilita, Tranquila and Serena,* ambitious definitions for modest lodging next to a busy road. Doug remembered that the new unit that the Williams
stayed in was named *Villa Romantico.* In order to get modern plumbing, decorative tiles and adequate lighting, Doug wrote that the new unit should have, "a
quality equal to or better than that found in Villa Romantico." He was trying to
close what he saw were glaring, if not deliberate, loopholes.

The document clearly stated that Pedro and Genie had the exclusive right to act
as agents to sell the property. Doug understood that Pedro could preserve the
integrity of the hotel if he controlled any future sale. It would be handled by a
corporation that had the magnanimous name of Santa Rita Realty. He winced at
the 10% agent's fee, but figured that it would insure a maximum effort by Pedro
to make a quick sale. Doug had called Pedro to get more detail on the clause
naming Eugenia as the *Presta Nombre.* Pedro explained that Genie, with her
Mexican citizenship, owned the Casa de Cabra land but could not sell it directly
to the Williams because they were foreigners. Therefore Genie would be a Presta
Nombre or a "Name Lender" to the Williams. Doug was assured that all of the
coastal land sold to Americans in Mexico was held in this manner. Nevertheless,

he wanted to nail down the idea that Enid was buying everything from the land up and that Eugenia Sessions was only a means to an end. He added these words.

"The purchasers shall have exclusive control over all aspects of the property and Isabella Eugenia Sessions shall have no rights including those to sell the property without the purchaser's authorization."

Doug purchased a soft cover book called *Surviving Mexican Laws*. It advised that any important document should be prepared in Spanish by a *Notario Publico* who seemed to be some kind of a title searcher, attorney and judge all wrapped into one. Doug requested that Pedro follow the requirement. Within a day, Doug's English version of the agreement was signed and faxed back and a Spanish version was sent the following week that looked very official with impressive official stamps on each page. A signed statement by a translator confirmed that the Spanish document was a true and accurate interpretation of the original English version. On the last page was a statement written in a different type face. Below it a larger circled imprint contained a cameo of a mustached official over the name: *Alberto de Silva Monterrey, Notario Publico, Santa Rita*. His signature was scrawled over the circle. By consulting the New World *Dictionario Español/ Inglés* the Williams confirmed that the two documents were very similar.

The agreement was set aside because of storms brewing in the Williams' relationship that were far worse than the winter gales of snow outside. The biggest problem between them involved Doug's second wife. When Doug moved to Steamboat, he agreed with Victoria to enroll their son in the Colorado Mountain Academy in Garfield County. This wasn't too far from Steamboat and would give Doug renewed contact with his heir. He hadn't counted on Victoria moving herself to Aspen as her legal residence "so that both of us could be near our boy." Enid knew little of this and was surprised to find soon after their marriage day that Doug was having numerous phone conversations with Victoria. When asked about them, Doug explained that Victoria was constantly calling to make sure he had mailed the monthly support check or to request additional funds for their boy. He knew that her list of necessary and verifiable expenses was well padded to insure Victoria of adequate funds to pursue a normal Aspen lifestyle.

Aspen soon became her former residence. Victoria came up with a different plan: her son should have the opportunity of going to an Eastern prep school like his father's. She of course must move to Pennsylvania "to be closer to the boy."

Doug didn't have the will to stop either plan and couldn't argue with the logic of having the Williams Trust invest in a Pottstown house in lieu of having to pay rent. The new association with a Philadelphia man she'd met skiing was never discussed.

The constant phone calls from Victoria annoyed Enid. She knew when they were married that Doug, like her, had children but she never anticipated that a former wife would need so much attention. In contrast to her dislike of Victoria, she was sympathetic to Doug's problems with his daughter from the first marriage. The girl, Lisa, had had multiple troubles. They began with the birth defects from her alcoholic mother, continued with reduced intelligence levels in her youth and expanded with excessive drug use during her teens. After years of therapy and halfway houses, she seemed to be stable and eager to start with a man she'd met at an AA 12-step meeting. Enid generously opened her home for their wedding.

A few months earlier, Mary Starman had opened the *Steamboat Jewelry Center*. It was, granted, a presumptuous name but there was no similar facility in the Springs. She had had a gala opening show featuring jewelry by a creative Southwest craftsperson and she reinforced the display with works by Colorado landscape artists. A side room held attractive Navajo-like rugs that few realized were manufactured in Romania.

Enid had been too tied up with Mexico and the wedding to spend much time at the store, even though she'd been called upon to pay bills for remodeling the shop space and purchasing some inventory. Soon after the wedding, Enid received a call from the superintendent of the art center building who was looking for the co-owner of *Steamboat Jewelry Center*. He wanted to know why the shop doors had been shut for a week and when the rent check for the last three months would arrive. Enid was baffled and asked the man to meet her at the mall because she did not even have a key to the space. As he unlocked the front door, she could immediately see that the walls were almost bare, the rugs removed and there was no sign of the jewelry. In the back office she found a pile of credit card receipts on the antique desk. Enid quickly put them in her purse. Mary Starman was not there. Mary Starman was not in her home. Mary Starman had skipped town.

Enid was trying to sort out the art gallery problem when a friend called to tell her that Victoria was returning to Colorado "to be near the boy" who was now attending the state college in Fort Collins. Victoria's reasoning seemed sound to Doug. In order for the boy to receive low, in-state college tuition rates, he needed to be a legal state resident. While living in Pennsylvania she had fooled the Colorado system with a drop box address in Aspen; but in order to keep the ruse from being discovered she was moving back again.

Victoria's phone calls to Doug became daily events. Whenever Enid accused Doug of spending far too much time accommodating Victoria, Doug turned away with obviously no intent to discuss the matter. Doug had just had such a session and was headed for the front door when he heard a ring from the large bronze cone that served as a doorbell. Doug opened the door to be greeted by two uniformed deputy sheriffs.

"Are you Douglas Williams?" After an affirmative answer from Doug, one of them continued with the familiar statement that began, "You have the right to remain silent...." Baffled and suddenly hit by an uncontrollable shaking, Doug was shuffled down the walk and into the Sheriff's car. In the Routt County jail he learned that he was being accused by Lisa and her new husband of theft from a supposed Trust Fund. They claimed that he'd stolen millions of dollars that were earmarked for taking care of Lisa's unique problems.

A baffled Douglas Williams sat in a county jail cell trying to understand what was happening to him. His shaking hands were a constant reminder of an ironic reality. A lifetime of keeping in good physical shape was now being rewarded with a bodily deterioration that would end in death. Why? No one could give him an answer. A Victoria that he'd faithfully supported was now thanking him by threatening his present marriage. His troubled first born daughter that he had supported, despite having no responsibility for her condition, had put him in jail. These worries weren't diminished by his lawyer's arrival to arrange a release on bail.

After processing the papers, the attorney sympathetically helped Doug into the front seat of his SUV and drove him back to his home. Doug thanked him and assured him that he was strong enough to make his own way to the front door. As his lawyer drove off, Doug noticed a manila envelope with his name on it pinned into the wood panel of the door. He slowly removed the envelope and read the first page of a long document.

When Enid heard the charges from the police officer and watched her husband being escorted away she immediately called Lisa for an explanation. Tearfully, with her husband coaching her in the background, Lisa explained the sins of her father that had been detailed in conferences between Lisa's new husband and his lawyer friend. This charge was just enough to push Enid beyond the boundary where marriage vows are respected. For months she had pondered a future of caring for a husband who was progressively getting worse. She was angered by his increasing acceptance of Victoria's presence in their life. She had discussed the situation with her own attorney that had prepared her for a final move. The papers that Doug found in his hands had a single message. Divorce!

Friends in Steamboat Springs could not believe the rumors. How could this gentle man, plagued with the oncoming signs of a deathly illness, be in such trouble? The story was soon expanded to "how could this nice couple be in such trouble?" In addition to the divorce proceedings, Enid found that she had been taken by Mary Starman who had convinced Enid to set up a joint credit card account and had charged thousands of dollars for her personal use. Moreover, she had created other credit card accounts on the strength of the first one. Enid had found the walls of the gallery bare because Mary had disposed of the paintings at fire sale prices and never paid a cent to the artists. All that was left were a few Romanian rug knock-offs that had been taken to her garage. Mary had learned to cook more than food at the gourmet school.

Doug's case went before a judge. The suit was declared invalid when the judge learned that the million-dollar trust fund was a tragic combination of Lisa's imagination and her husband's manipulations. Doug explained that a small inheritance had been willed to his daughter; but he, as executor, had used most of it to pay psychiatric and other related bills. Despite the judge's decision, Enid did not change her mind about the marriage or men in general.

13

At Casa de Mastil, Pedro looked for ways to increase his income and, hopefully, his stature. He was convinced that his boutique hotel needed to expand. Even if it grew by eight to ten units, he would still only need the one housemaid that now in his opinion loafed through the day cleaning the three rooms. With more rooms he could buy linen, toilet paper and soap in bulk and lower the per-room costs. The improved bottom line would mean enough new income to support a permanent desk clerk, freeing Pedro for more surfing time. Pedro envisioned life as a leader, not as a peon.

Although he had escaped from a potential jail sentence in California, Peter Oliver Sessions had not lost the desire to succeed as a person of wealth. He knew this meant making deals that involved risks. Like taking the biggest wave, there was always the chance of crashing; but in Mexico he knew that any rules of financial play that might impede him were almost non-existent. There would be no Real Estate Board or SEC looking over his shoulder. It was up to customers to watch out for themselves. It was understood around Santa Rita that the First Commandment for a participant in any financial transaction was, "Buyer Beware." Pedro counted on Gringos being so charmed by the temporary, tropical lifestyle that few would ever look at the fine print of any real estate document.

Pedro's thoughts about expansion became visions of building a real hotel, not just a few beds for rent. This idea required financing, but in Mexico there was no such thing as a bank mortgage loan or construction financing. He would have to find other sources. At first, he made daily rounds of the town, searching out clean-shirted tourists that might be potential investors. He offered a free Margarita and tour of his property but it captured few candidates. He had to look beyond the town.

Something else added to his desire to expand Casa de Mastil and his standing amongst his peers. At first he had no reaction to Genie's announcement that she had missed two periods. When he then realized that she was pregnant, he felt the pride of potency, but also saw how a prospective child might help his fundraising for the new project. Pedro reasoned that enough time had passed since his escape from California. Citations had been filed and judgments made against senior members of the firm, but he was too small a fish for the SEC to fry. He reasoned that most of his former clients and tennis-playing friends would have forgotten or at least forgiven his escape dash four years before. He needed to reopen old contacts and get to their money. It was time to ride on the expectations common to would-be grandparents. The thrill of a grandchild would give a valid excuse for Pedro to be welcomed back into the family.

The junior Sessions were received in Santa Monica with hugs from Pedro's mother. His father stood in the background avoiding any emotional display by quickly suggesting that they dine at the club. The four Sessions should have walked along La Mesa Drive and then up to the club entry, but it was after golfing hours so Peter Senior suggested that they take the short route across the fairways. Invading the territory was not considered proper without clubs and a caddy but Senior was flaunting his membership seniority in the Riviera Country Club.

The Mission style clubhouse stretched out on a bluff before them. They walked up a gravel path to the massive, carved oak front door. Good and bad memories came back to Pedro as he passed through the doorway and into the walnut-paneled lobby. He was thinking about his joy in escaping from all this by surfing at Dogtown when he made eye contact with a classmate from UCSB.

"My God, it's Peter! How are you Buddy? 'Heard you'd made it big in Baja!"

"Hi, Gary Woodward. It's great to see you again!"

Overlooking Gary's confusion about Mexican geography, Pedro suggested they get together for a drink after he'd dined with his family. In the men's bar he traded success stories with his classmate. Pedro's emphasis was on the climate and lifestyle of Santa Rita. He talked convincingly enough to get Gary to agree to come to Santa Rita with his wife and young son. On the President's birthday weekend, the Woodwards took a Mexicana flight from Los Angeles to Mexico City with a connection to Mazatlan.

After a bumpy arrival down the single runway, they walked into a hot and humid reception building and went through the tedious process of filling out custom's forms and then being questioned in Spanish by a full-bearded immigration officer that looked like Ché Guevara in his green twill uniform. Their final hurdle was to pass what looked like an old yellow traffic signal. They had to stop, punch a button and watch the light turn green. If it had been red they would have been delayed while all their baggage was hand frisked by another uniformed officer. This wasn't about security. It was about keeping as many Mexicans as possible employed.

The Woodwards were greeted by Pedro and Genie with smiles and welcoming words when they arrived at Casa de Mastil. From that moment, Pedro and Genie spent every possible minute with their guests. They offered them the taste wonders of local red snapper, fresh *camerones* and succulent local tomatoes. Pedro also drove them around town and compared each section of Santa Rita with the great and superior location of Casa de Mastil. He supplied them with surfboards and taught them how to wait for the best wave, to rise up and enjoy the thrill of near weightlessness as they rode its crest. He took them to nearby, tourist free beaches where he extolled the privacy, slow wave action for swimming and beautiful natural sands for sun bathing. He was very free with information, if not facts, about the hotel's rental income stream.

The Woodwards were captured by the weather and charm of the small village. Gary Woodward soon agreed to become a fifty-fifty owner for a new villa that would be part of the hotel. He would be the financier, while the Sessions would provide the land and construction management. Pedro carefully explained to Gary how to avoid the complications of foreigners owning property along the coast. All he needed to do was to sign a *Presta Nombre* agreement. Genie's Mexican citizenship would take care of the rest. The arrangement was sealed with a handshake. The new villa would be called *Tortuga,* after the migratory ocean turtles that laid their eggs in Santa Rita beach sands. Pedro described the near-holiday spirit when the town turned out to watch the new hatches make their way to the sea. *Tortuga* was built as a separate building up the hill from the original "garage" rooms.

Gary asked out of curiosity about a building permit, and he was assured that no one had ever needed one in Santa Rita. Actually, there was a national building permit process but it had never been operational in this remote village. For generations the town had been run by the Ejito, so much so that some locals joked about it as the Independent Nation of Santa Rita. Before starting *Tortuga,* Pedro had told the Ejito Chairman some of what he intended to do and in return received a nod of approval. The nod was rewarded with a five hundred Peso note that later appeared in a plain white envelope on his office desk.

Taking advantage of the apparently healed family wounds, Pedro and a pregnant Eugenia returned once again for a visit to Santa Monica. Although his stated purpose was to further bind the two families, he was also looking for more investors plus the chance to once again test the waves along the Venice shores. Encouraged by Genie to make a memory visit to Dogtown, he ran into Mike Connell, a classmate from the Studio School. Mike had moved west to work as a designer for the Los Angeles Department of City Planning. Pedro turned on his charm and went after Mike as if he were a prospective investor. His schmoozing involved lots of questions about personal history and facts that most people liked to talk about when asked. It was a winning approach that culminated with Pedro asking an unexpressed question.

"How can I use this guy?"

Mike told Pedro about his often boring work with a city bureaucracy. Pedro thought about how difficult it was for him to put design ideas on paper. Mike could help him as sort of an extra pencil hand. The conversation soon led into a glorious description of the beauties, both natural and feminine, that could be found in Santa Rita. Pedro added a list of the many projects that he knew were just waiting for a talented designer. That designer would have free reign to implement his ideas in a village where nothing was considered too unique or progressive. He urged Mike to become his partner in a limitless series of creative challenges.

Within a month. Mike had quit the security of his Los Angeles job, packed his surfing clothes and arrived as a stranger in Santa Rita. He became a permanent resident in the same bedroom once occupied by Susan Warner. Mike enjoyed the shy smiles of the local women and looked forward to the chance of more surfboarding. After a few days of absorbing atmosphere, Mike became restless and finally asked Pedro,

"When do we start on new plans? How about those for expanding the hotel?"

"Let's talk about it out there," answered Pedro, pointing to the distant break in the surf. Mike decided that Pedro wanted to talk privately about the project and, following his suggestion, met him with his board at the water's edge. The two paddled out to the point where the waves crested over a sand bar. After they had caught a few big ones, Mike asked again about plans. Sitting astride his board, Pedro answered him.

"I'm about to close on a new partnership that will fund a huge expansion. We will build villas up and down the hillside that will need all your creative abilities." When Mike began to speak, he was cut off.

"You must remember, Mike, that_this is what it's all about: Being able to come out here, catch the big waves, enjoy the best part of life. Everything else is just a distraction."

Mike was surprised by his former friend and current employer. The man jumped quickly from arm waving entrepreneurial talk into this laid back surfer's pose. He could drop from a deal-making zeal into a silent sulk without any apparent reason. The two traits were incompatible. Mike needed better direction.

"What should I do in the meantime?"

"I want you to learn more about my planning needs. Do you really understand the demands of the hotel business, what it takes to get a five star rating? No? I will make you the fulltime manager so that you will know it inside-out."

After a month at it, Mike found that his job was mainly to carry guest's baggage, help clean up the rooms and drive the Jeep to Mazatlan to pick up things for Eugenia. While Mike did the drudgery work, Pedro went surfing. This, of course, was the privilege of an aspiring feudal lord, even if his lodging facility wasn't breaking even on a forty percent occupancy rate.

Each time that Mike mentioned the new plans, Pedro had a different excuse for not starting them. He didn't mention two problems: he didn't own enough land for an expansion and didn't have any money to buy it. There was another issue. After completing the garage remodel and constructing the new *Tortuga,* Pedro was beginning to think of himself as an accomplished architect. Although he truly needed someone with Mike's training and experience, Pedro didn't want to admit anyone but himself into the design process. Just as quickly as he had lured Mike into his orbit, Pedro forgot why he'd hired him.

Mike Quit.

Pedro could quickly jump from dumping one person into snagging another. This time he hoped to catch Enid Williams. After a summer spent in seclusion at her family's fishing club in Upper Michigan, Enid had returned to Steamboat. She felt free from the stuttering steps, from the breaking noise of a dropped highball glass, from all those damned phone calls. She still pitied Doug's condition, but adding that to her own physical problems, she knew that staying together was not fair to either of them. She reflected,

"I might even falter sooner than him. Let that bitch suffer. She deserves the burden of his care for all the grief she'd caused. Without her constant interruption, we wouldn't have had the breakup. Blame it all on Victoria!" Despite her growing sense of relief, Enid wanted to get out of Steamboat for enough time to let the rumors die down and have their friends accept her independence. She saw the perfect place for refuge in a return to Santa Rita.

When Enid showed up alone one day at Casa de Mastil, Pedro and Genie were surprised. They had heard nothing from Enid or Doug Williams after coming to what they thought was an amicable agreement. Enid quickly explained the reasons for the impromptu silence. An explanation of her plight brought soothing hugs from both Sessions with appropriate expressions of sympathy for her troubles.

Enid explained that she had been visiting friends in San Miguel de Allende and had spent two weeks there learning "Card Game Spanish." The course taught her the essential *Power Verbs: I need, I want, I can, I like, I have, I'm going.* With these she could add an infinitive to make a sentence. Enid felt that it was important to learn some of the language so that she could revisit Santa Rita, but not so much that she'd become embroiled in local affairs. After her problems with Doug and Victoria she was happy to be floating in the limbo that was allowed to a temporary foreigner.

For three days, Pedro continued his display of understanding friendship that he thought might lead Enid to invest in his hotel. Enid wasn't fooled by the unctuous approach, but she liked the location and told Pedro that she might be interested in purchasing a new unit. Pedro produced a copy of the original purchase document and suggested that it would be valid if they deleted Doug's name. Enid authorized a wire transfer of $125,000 from Steamboat First Bank to Pedro's account with Bank of America in San Diego. With the money in hand, Pedro suggested that Enid might want to reconsider the site and she settled on one right below Casa Canto, the Sessions name for the Goat House. Here, the views of the entire bay were better and the prevailing westerly winds kept the site cool.

Enid was moved to better quarters in Gary Woodward's Tortuga and remained there in order to watch construction of her home. She envisioned her villa surrounded by flowering Hibiscus, Bougainvillea and Ginger plants and thought it should be named *Las Flores* but Pedro insisted that it was already officially listed as *Villa La Arboleda*.

Each day Enid climbed the 100 steps from Tortuga to the Casa Canto where she could observe the construction progress of La Arboleda. She watched an ancient back hoe scrape away the decomposed granite in order to establish a level site. The remaining ground preparation work was done by hand. At one time 6 men and boys labored with shovels to cut away the hillside while a 2 man team carried the cut material away in a battered wheel barrow. One held the handles while another pulled the barrow with a rudimentary rope harness.

Pedro appeared sporadically during the site preparation. He hoped to show that he was in charge by pulling out and resetting, only inches away, the stakes installed by Manuel. The stakes were the guidelines for trenches that were dug and shaped to receive concrete footings and foundations. A lumbering dump truck brought in long lengths of rusting reinforcing rods that were dropped at the top of the site. Enid watched as two of the crew bent the metal into shapes that were laid into the trenches and loosely tied together by wires.

She expected to see a large truck delivering ready-mixed concrete to form the foundations. Instead, some of the younger men were separated into teams and spelled each other at bursting open fifty pound sacks of dusty cement, adding sand and gravel brought in from the river and then mixing them all on the flat ground with water from a large, black plastic storage tank. The resulting mix was sloshed into 10 gallon buckets and poured into the open trenches. The process went on day after day and she wondered how the men felt about their task and what they talked about during a break. What would it be like to go home to wives and family and try to add importance to a description of the day's drudgery?

As soon as the concrete set up, a team of masons arrived to form walls out of concrete blocks and mortar. Each day, as Enid concentrated on watching the construction process, she was interrupted by Pedro's insistence upon describing his design ideas. She later described the scene.

"The little guy would wave his arms around, pointing here and there, without really saying much. You'd think he was building a palace for a Saudi prince!"

Enid could see the rows of concrete blocks grow to form almost sinuous curves that defined the different rooms. The free forms were so different from the familiar square or rectangular shapes she lived with in Colorado. In fact the whole operation was that way. There was no sheaf of blue-lined plans, no man checking levels with a transit atop a tripod, not even someone to watch out for construction flaws. Remembering the times that city officials came to check on construction of her home in Steamboat Springs, she asked Pedro,

"Where are the inspectors? Aren't they supposed to check off some kind of permit schedule and sign it after each visit?"

Pedro tried to work around an answer and finally told her that the permit was being processed. While building Tortuga, Pedro and Manuel had heard about the need for permits from one of the suppliers that brought cement and reinforcing rods to the site. The supplier complained that another job had been stopped and delivery orders cancelled because the builders hadn't obtained permits.

Pedro admitted to himself that perhaps telling the Ejito Chairman about his building wasn't enough, but he had a hatred for anything like a permit. Permits to him were the antithesis of why he was in Mexico in the first place. They were the first indication of someone imposing demands, limitations on his freedom of choice. Succumbing to such stricture would undermine the mental wall that he'd built against social codes, institutional rules, and his over-dominating father. Pedro couldn't live with someone else's boundaries. He relished his ruling status within the hotel, even if it was limited to ordering around a housekeeper and Manuel. He liked being the creator, the inspired artist shaping his own ideas into three dimensional realities. He loved being the only one to decide when he was going surfing and which wave to take that would carry him effortlessly to shore.

After listening to the supplier, he begrudgingly agreed with Manuel to drive to the county offices and get more facts about the system. There, Manuel found a clerk ready to issue Pedro a *Licensia de Construccion* on the spot, providing of course that Pedro paid him in cash for such rapid service. For twice the normal fee, the official looking document permitted a *"2 bedroom house at Casa de Mastil off Camino Accesso."* It was undated. Pedro could then fill in the date for any 2 bedroom project at Casa de Mastil. He drove away smiling about his skills with *soborno.* Such bribery was still the easiest way to do business with the government. Although hardly what might be expected from an Evangelical Christian, this moral lapse came from his belief that payoffs were the normal Mexican way of rewarding a favor. The system in Mexico was just different from that in the US. Money was required for results in both countries. It was just channeled in a different way.

Genie always tried to distance herself from Pedro's business operations. She only became involved in the early phases of each deal because she had to sign purchase agreements as the future *Presta Nombre.* At meetings with potential buyers she dutifully displayed an outward charm and friendliness, but she tactfully avoided detailed business conversations. When faced with what seemed like strange or questionable terms in a given agreement that she had to cosign, she might ask her husband about them. He typically responded,

"It's a necessary way to do business here in Mexico."

Pedro, Genie and young son left for a two week's visit to Santa Monica. Despite his absence at a critical point in La Arboleda's construction, his departure didn't bother Enid. She'd lost any embarrassment about her poor Spanish and found ways to communicate her wishes to Manuel. Although she knew she was bypassing Pedro, she began to point at things and refer to her English/Spanish dictionary for the correct translation. She saw that electrical boxes hadn't been located in spots where they would be used. She explained to Manuel that the switches were all placed in the middle of a room close to the outlets and not near door openings where you needed them. Outlets for lamp plugs were at mid-height on a wall rather than placed near the floor. Outlets in the kitchen were found in hard-to-reach places under the counters. Enid thought about it.

"Of course, how could he possibly understand the problem when he probably didn't have electricity in his own home?"

She learned from Manuel that Pedro had instructed him to build prominent archways through the walls on both sides of the living area. One led to the guest bedroom. She'd assumed that the other would lead into the Master Bedroom until she saw the plumber installing a 4 inch waste pipe directly opposite the arched opening. It was one of her more difficult moments with Manuel when she had to point out that the grand entrance focused on what would be a bright, white American Standard water closet. Manuel didn't understand her problem. He had just installed his first indoor plumbing at his own casa and was proud that he could show it off from his living area. Confused, but anxious to satisfy the Senora, he moved the opening so that it led directly into the bedroom.

It was an important milestone when the walls of La Arboleda were finished and the circular spaces of the bedrooms and kitchen were ready to receive their roofs. Pedro had proudly promised that the roofs would be brick domes, constructed by the most expert masons in the country. Enid watched one morning as an ancient Chevrolet station wagon appeared and disgorged six weary occupants that had driven from *Guanajuato* during the night. Soon, a load of red bricks arrived. Enid expected to see elaborately engineered formwork to hold the brickwork until the cement mortar had set up, so she watched in disbelief as rough wooden saw horses were set in place to support four or five loose planks. This provided a platform level at mid-height in each circular enclosure.

A single mason stood on each platform and placed the first row of bricks on top of the curving walls. Mortar was made up on the bare ground outside by the younger men who carried their mixtures in re-cycled five gallon cans to the masons. Then, the masons added a second row that projected slightly inward from the first row. From various points along the perimeter, bricks were laid to gradually shape the domed ceiling. There was no complicated scaffolding, no elaborate equipment. The only tool beside a mortar trowel was a single wire nailed roughly in the middle of the floor. By always making sure that each brick was a wire-length away from the center, a mason could produce a hemisphere with a uniform radius. The secret lay in the mason's knowledge of when the very-rich mortar had set enough to hold a brick in place before the next row was installed. As the sloping walls of the domes reached for closure, they met in perfect match and Enid now had three rooms with what were called *Boveda* ceilings.

The masons that had slept on the concrete floor of the villa and cooked their sparse meals on a mesquite campfire departed as silently as they had arrived. The next day a father, son and two daughters arrived with a large truckload of skinned wood poles and newly-cut palm fronds. The plumber, Paulo, who was Mexican by birth but had spent many years up north, came over to watch the operation. He surprised Enid by greeting her in English and then offering an explanation of how the family team was going to work.

"They are going to build a *Palapa* from the sticks and the palm fronds. The best fronds come from the tallest of the palm family, the Royal palms."

Enid was surprised by the impromptu approach but then thrilled to find that someone on the job spoke her language. He continued:

"The palm branches are cut in the middle of the night when they are more......pliable. Watch how the fronds will be run up and down and over the small struts. In cheaper palapas the fronds run the other way." Enid thanked him for the information as he turned away from her to return to his work. She watched them construct her palapa.

A single pole guyed with ropes was erected in the center of the living area and the young son shinnied up to its top. Clinging there, he lashed on smaller poles that reached out as radii to the concrete block walls. The father then cut and placed small wood struts between the radial poles and the daughters began to lace the palm fronds over and in between the struts to form a leak-proof roof. The fronds ran up and down as predicted by Paulo. Their work was finished in a day.

There was much more to be done: the application of plaster over the concrete block, the finishing of the rough concrete floors, the selection of paint, plumbing and light fixtures and the installation of doors. Enid would leave most of that to Manuel and hope that Pedro wouldn't order any changes in <u>her</u> villa.

14

Enid returned to Steamboat after watching the palapa go up at La Arboleda. In Colorado the Aspens had survived their autumn disrobing. Their new foliage glowed as if painted with Leaf Green squeezed directly from an artist's tube. Enid had left Santa Rita with a number of questions that she should have asked Pedro. What colors would he use in the different spaces? Were the sinks going to be hand painted like the ones she saw in Dolores Hidalgo? Would he put in wrought iron chandeliers? What about furniture selection? When could she move in? It looked to her as if the project could be finished in a month or two.

She had a major concern that seemed to confirm Enid's assessment of Pedro's guile. Her contract called for her to receive all rights to the land in question. She assumed that her villa would consist of a single floor above that land, yet somehow Pedro had shoved in a second level. What was going to happen with all that extra space? She faxed the questions to Santa Rita.

Pedro had learned from the murder incident that he should never commit anything to paper that might backfire. Feigning a lack of typing skills and a horror for the complexities of the new computers, he always used the telephone. Two days later he called Enid, first apologizing that his delay in answering her message was primarily due to all the time that he had to spend overseeing construction on her villa.

"You will be amazed to see how beautiful Villa La Arboleda is becoming. We now have on the Boveda roofs and have built the palapa."

Enid responded, "I know all that. I was there when it happened. What about all my questions?"

"Don't worry, my dear, I'll take care of everything you've asked for including the only private telephone in Santa Rita. You'll love it. You'll be ecstatic!"

Enid was so distracted by what seemed to be an obvious evasion that she almost forgot her most important question. She finally asked,

"What do you plan to do with all that space below my villa floor?"

He hesitated and then said," There's room there for a separate unit and storage space. I've always planned that to be part of the hotel. It is hewn out of the hard sandstone. I think I should call it La Roca."

Enid didn't like suddenly being told that what she thought was going to be her private villa was turning into multifamily housing. She didn't want to have to deal with arguments about who was responsible for what if the building was jointly owned. She had too many friends in Steamboat that continually complained about their condominium woes. She also quickly realized that, because the walls and ceiling were already in place to carry her villa, she would be paying for most of his La Roca. She challenged Pedro,

"You sold me a single villa on a piece of land and now you say you are going to steal the space below me. That isn't in our agreement. It specifically says that I own all the rights to the land." Pedro knew that he had to change his reasoning.

"I don't believe that the agreement recognized that in order for me to give you the best possible views, I had to raise the floor level. This created a big space below. I was going to keep the unit for myself but, if you want it.............it will cost another $100,000."

"I'll call you back." Enid really couldn't do anything else, except order him to drop the floor, and for that she'd have to forfeit her excellent views. She thought about what stocks she could sell and finally agreed to the added cost. When she called him back she asked,

"Will it be finished soon?"

"Oh we want to do everything just right. I can assure you that it will be finished on time."

What he didn't admit was that he had just received a large deposit for a new villa near Tortuga and was moving his crews over there to demonstrate rapid progress to the new buyers. The new customers were getting the full Pedro Sessions attack. He could forget Enid. She had been hooked. What was most important to Pedro was the 50% deposit from the new buyers because this was free cash in his pocket. All he needed was the next new buyer with a similar deposit to pay for labor and materials on the first two villas. If the project took longer and cost more than he'd estimated, he'd stiff the suppliers and promise his labor force they would be paid as soon as he'd gotten a new deposit for a third villa. Pedro was becoming expert at using other people's money.

Summer in Steamboat Springs was the best season of the year. Locals said,

"They come here for the skiing, but they stay because of summer!"

In June the Steamboat garden club put up a huge tent where they sponsored a series of chamber music concerts. In July the focus was on the big Fourth of July parade and Lion's Club Pancake Breakfast held in the park. A banner strung between two trees proclaimed, *All ya kin eat en then sum! $5.00.* If the garden club lost money on the music concerts, they planned to recoup the deficit in August with an annual event that opened the homes and gardens of the more affluent residents. As the secretary of the garden club, Enid felt obliged to be there for the house tour.

She returned to Mexico after the August event. Upon arrival she was faced with Santa Rita's summer heat and monsoon rains and stunned to see that literally nothing had been done on her villa since she'd left in the spring. In contrast, the great palms next door had been replaced with a new building. These palms were part of the green landscape that gave Pedro a plausible reason for naming her villa La Arboleda. Now he had cut down three major trees. In their place was a villa called……. *Tres palmas.*

Next to Tres palmas was an enclosure made out of rusting corrugated metal and dirt splattered plywood sheets. A TV aerial stuck up from its roof, attached with rusting bailing wire. A day's washing hung on a nearby clothesline, and a large hen herded six chicks away from the enclosure. She learned from Paulo that this was the temporary home of the project watchman, his wife and two small children. Enid didn't begrudge the temporary neighbors but she did resent being roused every morning by their rooster.

Pedro was juggling his construction crew between the two new villas, depending upon which buyer needed to be pacified by showing progress. The pacification was necessary to keep the progress payments flowing. Upon Enid's arrival, a dozen men appeared to resume work on her villa. Electricians cut away at the concrete blocks to make the changes she'd asked for in the spring. Plasterers covered the block walls with cement and added a colored finish coat. The rough concrete floors were smoothed over with integrally colored cement. Enid watched a skilled craftsman make an inlay pattern of stones and tiles that looked surprising like a circular rug permanently inscribed in the living area floor.

Enid was delighted to see the unusual features but could not understand why a large ceramic plaque decorated with trees and the words, Villa La Arboleda, had been hidden in the master bathroom. The artwork was plastered into the shower wall. It bore the signature, *Capelo*. Enid sought out Paulo to ask him if he knew where the plaque had come from.

"I've seen it sitting in a Bodega, a storage place, ever since I've been here. I guess he bought it at a sidewalk sale." She now knew why the project couldn't be called Villa Las Flores!

Enid was wondering more about Pedro's dual personality. She couldn't figure out how this shrewd manipulator could equally wear the mask as an architectural romantic. She asked others that knew him,

"What motivates the man?" Their answer was usually,

"I don't know and neither does he!"

One of Pedro's naive design ideas was that handrails on balconies spoiled views. He simply left them out. Enid threatened to withhold a payment if he didn't install a waist-high railing to keep people from tumbling to the ground. She couldn't agree, however, in the way that Pedro had followed her request for the small pool. She wanted it so that it would be filled to the top of the outside leading edge, blending the waters of pool and ocean into a single view. Instead of building a simple gutter to catch the overflow, Pedro had an artisan produce an elaborate bas-relief fashioned after an ancient Aztec sun symbol. He said that when water flowed over the pool edge it would splash prettily down over the sun sculpture into a series of catch pools. Pumps would send the gathered water back up to the pool. Enid would soon find out that he'd forgotten something.

As the October deadline for finishing La Arboleda got closer, workers were on the job from sunup to sundown. Finally, the noise of their early morning hammering ended. On the last day of September, the hotel staff was conscripted to move furniture, dishes, glassware and wall hangings into Villa La Arboleda. They worked far into the night and on the following morning Enid was invited for an inspection of the completed work. She could not hide her dismay as she walked into her villa. In the entrance patio, where she had expected brick paving like that at Romantico, sod grass had been hastily thrown down to cover the bare dirt surface. Laid into the grass were large, uneven stepping stones that were sure to trip up some of her more feeble friends. A wrought iron entrance gate framed the vista to the bay and distant points of land. It was captivating but gave her a problem. There was no closure to block off the strong westerly winds. Inside, Pedro had slopped sea foam green paint over every wall. It reminded her of hospital corridors.

The purchase agreement that both Pedro and Enid had signed specifically stated that the quality level of La Arboleda would be equal to or better than that found in Romantico. Enid couldn't believe that there could be such a difference. Whereas she had expected the same Mexican *Equipale* chairs and tables that were in Romantico, her living area looked like the afterbirth of a rummage sale. Facing the entrance gate was a settee covered in a soiled buff fabric that would have been more appropriate in the entry room of an Amsterdam brothel. Roughly-made wooden slat chairs had been covered with hastily-sewn, white canvas to hide the layers of peeling paint applied before their former owners tossed them out of their *casuchas*. Threatening the entire setting was a chandelier hanging from the top of the palapa. It reminded her of the steel toothed harrows that farmers used to break up the soil.

Pedro put on his former stockbroker's smile to say,

"Don't you love my mix and match?"

"I was expecting it to look like Romantico with traditional Mexican furniture. No, I don't like it."

"My dear, we have a Bodega filled with great pieces. Let's go peek in at them."

He led her to one of the rooms in the former garage. It was now filled with a variety of furnishings. Enid spotted an old armoire that could be used to house her music and video. She pointed to it and then to two marble-topped side tables and a matching round table that would be good for dining, two lamps with turned wood bases, a standing iron lamp and a leafy iron chandelier.

"I would like that and those and that and those and that and that!"

"Well, I could give you the tables, but the chandelier has been saved for a new villa."

"If you want a final payment, you'd better send those up to my villa and also find some traditional Mexican chairs that someone can sit on."

Pedro realized that he had a problem.

"You can't imagine how hard I tried to make Villa La Arboleda a showplace! Mexican furniture is all filled with bugs—termites—and falls apart in this moist atmosphere. If you don't want what I've picked out you might find something in Mazatlan. Better still at *Adobe* in Guadalajara. I have an account there." He hoped that she would balk at going all the way to Guadalajara.

Enid was just angry enough to rent a car from Avis in Mazatlan and follow highway 200 to Compostela. There she picked up the two-lane toll road that carried her into the mountains and connected her in Chapallila with the four-lane *Cuota*. The toll road ran through lava beds formed from ancient volcanic eruptions and then it climbed to a mountain pass. As she descended she passed hillsides planted with purple and green Agave plants whose roots were boiled to produce the liquor that was becoming popular with younger drinkers in the States. She had seen ads for the liquor and was surprised to find it was actually produced in a town called Tequila.

Her destination, the shop called Adobe, wasn't in Guadalajara but in the difficult to pronounce suburb of Tlaquepaque. There she found that the one-time summer homes of affluent, early Spanish families in Guadalajara had been turned into restaurants and antique furniture shops. Their elegant stone fronts lined *Camino Independencia* that was now limited to pedestrian traffic.

In front of Adobe was a giant Equipale chair that dwarfed the child sitting in it while her tourist father took a picture for his travel scrapbook. Once inside she found that Adobe was a combined store and restaurant. Patrons heading for the dining room were surrounded by artifacts. Raffia baskets were filled with fruits formed from colored papier-mâché. Enid saw deer sculpted out of rusted, flattened tins and small bugs with bodies made from salvaged spark plugs as she headed for the furniture department. There she was quickly asked if she'd like assistance and soon settled on four Equipale chairs, diminutive versions of the one near the front door. The chairs had leather seats held up by a latticework of criss-crossed wood slats. All the parts were held together by leather thongs. She also found a teak cupboard that would help make up for Pedro's failure to provide any lockable storage space.

At the charge desk she asked that the pieces be delivered to her in Santa Rita and that, with the proper fifty percent discount, they be billed to Pedro Sessions at Casa de Mastil. The request was met with a discouraging stare.

"We are sorry that we cannot do that. Mr. Sessions has a long overdue balance with us." Enid asked to use the phone. She called Pedro and explained the problem. He told her, in a very disgruntled tone, that there was obviously some mistake. He would correct it as soon as he could find out what happened to the check that he was sure he'd signed within the week. He advised Enid to pay cash or use a credit card.

"I'll promptly reimburse you." Enid was beginning to better understand Pedro's way of manipulating people and financial obligations. She answered him with,

"No, I'm not able to do that. They have agreed to hold everything for me and deliver them to Santa Rita as soon as they receive your payment."

A disappointed Enid made her way back to the coast. She was happy to return to a cooling ocean breeze but really annoyed after her next conversation with Pedro. At first he refused to pay for the sideboard and then grumbled about the entire purchase price. He knew that he had to go through with his offer. He'd already removed the objectionable pieces from La Arboleda and placed them in one of his other recently completed units. This left Enid with no place to sit down. She waited two weeks for Pedro to act, listening to a stream of excuses.

"We need to investigate their false claims about an unpaid balance."

"We only cut checks on the first and fifteenth of the month."

Enid was beginning to mark the measure of the man but was not quite sure on which scale or in what category.

15

Enid was enjoying the sunshine on the deck of Villa La Arboleda. Hidden under a large woven hemp hat, she thought about how pleasant it was to spend the winter months in her new villa. Free of Doug's desire to be there during ski season, she was happy that the snow and cold of Steamboat were some 1400 air miles away.

She was never again smothered by Pedro's or Genie's unctuous hugs. They abandoned her after she made her final payment. Anything she learned about the Sessions came from watching the construction or chance meetings with guests or other owners on the beach. She heard that Pedro had found a new financial partner. The owner of Tortuga, Gary Woodward, was receiving a generous cash flow from his share of the rents. He was assured by Pedro that, if he kept the funds in Mexican pesos, there was no need to report them on his US income tax returns. Further, as a non-resident foreigner he didn't have to pay any taxes in Mexico. Gary had made enough to deposit 300,000 pesos in Pedro's Lloyds Bank account. He agreed to come up with another 300,000. This gave him a 50% share of a partnership that would build two houses on the hillside east of town.

Pedro insisted that, as the developer, he needed to be able to draw freely from the joint account. When Gary agreed, Pedro immediately took $40,000 out of the account to repay himself for the land even though that was supposed to be part of Pedro's contribution to the partnership. The hoped-for sales price of each house was set at $275,000. Pedro would also pay himself 10% of this sales price before splitting the remaining balance with Gary. To start the project, the hillside site was bulldozed to make a platform for the foundations. Dirt was pushed down the hill and the resulting erosion during the summer rains destroyed a huge tree below their property. The tree itself wasn't as important as the fact that it was home to a four foot long Iguana. Pedro shrugged off criticism. There was no profit in saving the environment.

The first of the two villas to be finished was kept in the partnership to be rented for the time and, hopefully, peddled for a high price in the future. The second villa was sold to a fellow member of Gary's golf club. He arrived for his first vacation in Santa Rita to find water flowing from a faulty connection below the villa. He shut off a main valve that stopped the waste, but soon found out that he had shut off the water supply to both houses. Pedro had tied both villas to the same water meter in order to save on connection fees. In a perverted sense of sharing, Pedro had also put in one septic system to serve both villas. Neither villa could fill or flush without depending upon the other.

Pedro had agreed that Casa de Mastil would provide the villas with daily maid and maintenance service. The first tenant to rent villa number one found on arrival that the pool wasn't filled and beds were unmade. After a week, the electricity was turned off because the power company found out that Pedro had connected two dwellings to the same meter, again to save on connection fees. Despite the renter agreeing to reduce the promised daily cleaning days to two times a week, personnel still failed to show up. After two weeks the friend moved out and tried many times to telephone Pedro in order to have his $4,500 rental deposit refunded. Pedro was never there to take the calls, ducking out either to surf or promote his new project.

Another story that Enid heard was that Pedro had discovered a rectangular lot of four hectares for sale in nearby Santa Cruz. The long side was ocean frontage. He began verbal negotiations with the landowner, suggesting a partnership to develop the land. Before any formal agreement had been made with the landowner, Pedro had a scaled map of the land prepared. It showed a road down the back of the property that would serve 16 detached villas along the waterfront. A potential buyer that showed up at Casa de Mastil looking to buy beach frontage was told about the new project. This was a time when the cost of beachfront property in California was approaching 15,000 dollars a front foot. There was only so much coastline in the world and each year its value increased.

When he was shown the land, the man was sure that he had discovered a new Carmel. He made a $50,000 deposit to secure a lot. He was told that a *Certificado Parcelario* identified Genie as the legal owner of the property and thus capable of selling its rights. Pedro assured the man that the title papers had been processed and copies were in his safe deposit box in California. After a year of Pedro promising to supply the documents but never delivering them, the purchaser went to review whatever he could find at the county recorder's office. There he was shown a Certificado for the parcel. The Certificado was in the name of Carlos Ramirez, the real owner of the land. It never belonged to Eugenia. To Enid's knowledge the $50,000 was never repaid.

At Casa de Mastil, Enid had to admit that Pedro's unusual design ideas were being translated into buildable reality by Manuel, the creative, and now the general, contractor. The hotel complex had developed a distinctive character. Small villas painted in muted tones of rust and ochre stepped up the hillside. Some had Boveda domes painted an azure blue. They were all surrounded by native plants that gave a sense of separateness to individual units but an overall tapestry of communal green. Pedro had produced an elegant sense of privacy within an active, operating hotel. Its charm was verified by guest testimonials and in complimentary paragraphs in *Foders* guidebook and *Travel* magazine. Pedro's limited design training and his inability to draw straight walls had surprisingly produced a place where people wanted to visit or even become owners.

The *Travel* magazine publicity attracted a couple from Telluride, Colorado that wanted to be near the water. They also needed an easy, level access for an infirmed relative. Manuel was told to build them a villa similar to Enid's on a site that had the level access. Two Boveda ceilings covered bedrooms and a flat concrete ceiling was placed over the living area. Across an open deck an isolated palapa sheltered a third bedroom. Pedro christened it, "The Shepard's Cottage."

The new purchasers were impressed by Pedro's convincing description of his performance on the other villas so that they didn't worry when business demands kept them from visiting the growing project. In fact they never got the chance before its completion. When they finally arrived for a housewarming visit, they found that the parking space promised for the invalid access was covered with sod grass and separated from the road with a series of posts and metal fencing. In addition, the 30 amp main power panel was insufficient to serve the building. Plumbing vents were missing so that fumes from the sewer pipes rose into the shower and wash basin drains. These errors might have been caught by an inspector if a legitimate building permit had been issued. Pedro, of course, avoided such an inconvenience.

Casa de Mastil lacked a common connector. Although a brick stairway had been built by Emilio, a name the Sessions wanted to forget, that stair led directly from Casa de Cabra to the former garage. Pedro decided that a stairway along the western property line would not only tie the overall hotel project together but it could become a structural feature. Pedro was thinking about a stairway that curved back and forth up the hill: the kind of steps where models could pose for publicity shots. To Pedro, this seemed like an obvious operation. Steps were steps. To Manuel it was a new challenge because he, like most other Mexicans in Santa Rita, had few causes to use steps. The buildings in Santa Rita were single storied. To go up and down a hill, one just followed the dirt paths that had been grooved in over time. If Pedro had had better training he would have known that proper steps had to be identical to keep the user from miss-judging their dimensions and ending up with a trip and fall. An empirical guideline stated that the sum of the riser and the flat part of the step, the tread, should always equal 17 and1/2 inches. Thus a 7 inch riser and a 10 ½ inch tread or a 6 inch riser and an 11 ½ inch tread. Once established for a given stair the ratio could not be changed. In addition, there should be handrails all along the stairway to assist travel or avoid a fall.

Manuel knew none of this and Pedro's limited technical knowledge and increasing absence from the work wasn't a help. They both agreed that the new steps should be made out of concrete and Manuel set his crew to work. From the beach road to the first villa the ascent was steeper and the masons instinctively made them with about 8 inch risers, although the dimension varied from step to step. Most building codes stated that there should be no more than fifteen steps between level platforms. Manuel made 20 steps to reach the first villa. Similar results were produced all the way to the top of the hill. Proud of their work, the masons finished off each step with concrete that was burnished to perfection. It glowed! The new stairway was the largest piece of concrete work in all of Santa Rita, but its 152 steps had no railings.

Enid made the climb from the beach road without event each day that she walked to the ocean or the village. Others were not so fortunate and one person that tripped and fell on the slick steps filed a lawsuit. The suit acknowledged that Mexican laws about stairways were probably non-existent; but North Americans using the stairways in Mexico expected the same standard of care that they experienced at home. Pedro had developed an attitude about these lawsuits. They were only games for the lawyers, but in order to fight the current suit he returned to the *Abrogado* that had represented him in the murder case. His attorney's first advice was to immediately get a blanket liability insurance policy for Casa de Mastil. To pay for this, Pedro simply deducted $1800 from the rents due each owner. This was to cover the cost of their privilege in sharing what were obviously his risks. The only explanation for the charge was the word "Insurance" opposite the $1800 charge on the quarterly statement of income and expenses.

Enid balked, because she already had a policy with Lloyd's that covered her risks when she was in La Arboleda. Her agreement said that at other times Pedro was liable for accidents that happened whenever he placed renters in the villa. When she insisted upon an $1800 refund from Pedro, Lloyds mysteriously cancelled her policy because, they said, they had not known that the villa would be rented out. Enid couldn't see how Lloyds had been prompted to cancel until a helpful clerk told her it was because they knew she would be included under a new blanket insurance coverage. They were just in the process of writing up such a policy for Casa de Mastil.

Soon thereafter Enid received another call from Lloyd's, this time from a very friendly account manager. Enid was told that they would be happy to re-write Enid's policy to include protection during renter occupancy. She learned the reason why. Lloyds had invested many hours and pesos in preparing the policy that Pedro had requested. Pedro then used it as a target to shop for lower bids from others. Her new policy with Lloyds increased her premium to $900.00, just half of what Pedro had tried to charge her.

Enid reviewed her position with Pedro as she lounged in a deck chair near her pool. Over the two years she had paid him extra dollars, always in advance, to bring her villa up to a reasonable standard of completion. She had added her own teak pool furniture. She installed a door to make at least one of the open storage areas into a lockable closet. On her many visits to the *vivero* in Santa Cruz she bought bright red geraniums, multi-colored hibiscus and rust colored bougainvillea to turn Pedro's haphazardly planted patio garden into a true flowering *Arboleda*.

On the good side, she could sit in her living area and still be enchanted by her ocean view. It could change in one day from flat calm into heavy waves thumping in even cycles on the rocky shore. In mid-winter, while bears and chipmunks hibernated in Colorado, dolphin and hump-backed whales invaded Santa Rita bay. She marveled at the pelicans and heermann gulls that turned the sea white as they hovered over a school of bait fish. Overhead, frigate birds and hawks circled slowly in the updrafts, searching for food below. She loved her villa and had to credit Pedro and Manuel for the collection of romantically shaped buildings they invented to climb between palms and ficus trees to the top of the hill.

All of the good things about La Arboleda, however, were offset by a new situation that made Enid more suspicious of Pedro Sessions. Her gardener was fired for supposedly stealing a hose. When the friendly and capable maintenance man failed to show up to clear a blocked drain, she was told that the man was caught smoking a cigarette on the job. With his demise, power suddenly shut down, phone lines went dead and faucets were dripping because he was the only one that knew how the systems worked. The constant shuffle of service people frustrated Enid. Maids and gardeners would just get to know her likes and dislikes when they would be replaced by new, typically inexperienced workers.

It was impossible to confront Pedro with a complaint about the ever-changing staff because Pedro and Genie were moving away. Their public excuse was that their growing son needed to be closer to a good private school. They said that buying a small condominium in Punta Viento would obviate the daily trip through the jungle that took two hours each way out of Genie's day. The distance from Punta Viento to the school was actually about equal to that from Santa Rita, so that explanation didn't fool Enid. She saw the move as a way that Pedro could have a new playground of moneyed vacationers that might just also be players in the Casa de Mastil game. He could rub shoulders with the rich, and have his hand in their pockets at the same time.

The Punta Viento Golf Club and Resort commanded the beach and took over most of the once-jungled property at the western end of the point. The thick tropical foliage had been cleared away and replaced by small casitas. Behind their orange facades, 140 hotel rooms were grouped along the fairways of a Jack Nicklaus golf course. Guests, even Sheiks and Hollywood stars, were stopped at the guarded entry gate until their reservations were verified by phone from the front desk. Once allowed in they could dine in two different restaurants, play on the four tennis courts, or use the fitness machines. They could get bodies renewed at the spa or swim and surf at the exclusive, private beach. Few knew or cared that before the gates were installed this just happened to be one of the best public access surfing beaches in the state.

A visitor with the poise of Peter Oliver Sessions was quickly welcomed at this recently opened resort hotel. They provided him with a reduced rate tennis club membership in hopes that he might attract others to fill the meager roster. This allowed him to tour the grounds in anticipation of finding more investors for his various, unfinished projects. At the tennis courts he found a willing opponent in the tennis pro, Jeff Woods. Jeff found that few guests wanted lessons and he was happy to offset the boredom.

Pedro was careful to play only the most sportsmanlike tennis and praise Jeff's more skillful shots. At a break between sets, Pedro told Jeff about Casa de Mastil and his dreams to make his hotel an equal to Punta Viento resort. Just as he scrutinized everyone he met, Pedro was trying to figure out how he could use Jeff. He knew there wasn't money there but he invited him to visit Santa Rita. Pedro stood with him on the top of the bluff. He described how the remaining land below would be built out to complete a setting of exclusive villas that together would form a boutique retreat. He convinced him that great opportunities abounded in Santa Rita and then, as almost an afterthought, said that there was an opening for a new manager at Casa de Mastil. He did not tell him why the last manager had left.

Jeff gradually learned about Pedro's unique hiring practices and his way of complying with national rules and regulations on employment. Pedro did tell him that the hotel's original workforce consisted of local teen-age girls and retired fishermen and how he sometimes had to unhappily dismiss pregnant women whose condition might be threatened by the work. Naturally, any drinkers were fired on the spot. He admitted that, given the nature of the workforce, some incompetents or pilferers were dismissed after a few months of work and others just drifted away after receiving their first few real paychecks. Jeff soon learned that the unordinary turnover was purposely engineered. Pedro may have been unschooled about building codes but he was an expert on employment law that said that after a reasonable period of evaluation, every employee must be paid the minimum wage set by the government for each state.

Every employee was entitled to twice this wage for overtime work, a vacation with pay, an annual bonus and Severance Pay if fired without cause. Pedro didn't want to pay these ridiculous additions to what he believed was a fair wage. He made sure that there was always a cause for dismissing even the best of employees after they had been there for six months. If they stayed any longer, he would have to pay all the benefits required by the government.

The new manager and former tennis pro could not accept Pedro's callous system. He had had little experience in personnel management but common sense told him that he needed to have employees that had some prior experience and they needed incentives to stay with the job. Jeff went to Pedro, insisting that he have the right to hire and fire. Pedro grimaced at the thought of losing control, but knew he'd have to give in or lose another manager. The alternative would only lead to more complaints from Enid and return management tasks to Pedro. He didn't want to lose any more time working when he could be surfing.

Pleased with the decision, Jeff hired away key workers from Punta Viento Resort that knew how to tighten up operations. They were offered the same pay, but more responsible positions and the chance to move up in the future. Forced to accept the changes in staff and their inevitable extra costs, Pedro demanded that Jeff make up for the added expense by short-cutting operations. A time-clock was installed in the former surf-board storage room. It was re-named the Employee Lounge. A morose Maria took over as Housekeeper. An authoritative Oscar was installed as Concierge and Reservations Clerk.

Despite the initial confusion from the change, Pedro liked the way Jeff had applied Punta Viento systems to Casa de Mastil. It allowed him to be less involved with daily operations and avoid customer complaints. Jeff also brought with him ideas that added "class." He had the Casa de Mastil logo stamped into soap bars and embroidered on hand towels. A small sticky-back label with the logo held the lead tissue on a roll of toilet paper from untimely unraveling. The theft-proof closet hangers were replaced with mahogany takeaways bearing the hotel name. Terry cloth robes with a **CM** sewn over the breast pocket hung in each closet. Each night a cherry-flavored chocolate wrapped in silver and red foil was placed on a pillow. The candy gift was short-lived. Enid discovered why on a weekly trip to Sam's Club. Pushing her cart along with the many other Norte Americanos that were buying liquor and steaks, she noticed the silver and red wrapped sweets in one gallon jars. A card had been placed above the candy that said the sweets were no longer on sale.

Enid found more disappointments. She noticed that a large drain pipe extended down below the La Roca ceiling. Pedro had disguised it with plaster shaped to look like a large bamboo log. He refused to spoil this illusion with a conventional U-shaped trap that would have kept waste fumes from passing up the pipe. Instead, Pedro's "wet" vented system pushed assorted excreta smells back into her shower and washbasins. Each morning Enid threw a wet wash cloth over the drain opening. Each noon a meticulous maid removed it.

There were other water problems. The cascading overflow from her pool proved to be a magnificent mistake. Water that splashed over the pool edge was collected in the two smaller pools below. Because the flow was only intermittent, the pools turned into stagnant breeding grounds for mosquitoes. The tainted water could not be recycled back without polluting the pool. The list grew. In La Roca, Pedro had installed a washbasin without an overflow. One unfortunate guest mistakenly left on a faucet. Her understandable error caused a flood that ruined most of her clothes and made the space un-rentable for a week.

The entrance to La Roca was an old door from Pedro's stockpile of "antiques." The portal scrounged from a junk yard came with termites that munched at the wood panels until they were paper-thin. To heighten the sense of La Arboleda as a wooded place Pedro had built a small waterfall that trickled into a rock-rimmed pool. He turned on the re-circling pump whenever he passed by. Within minutes, the water running down the porous rock wall behind the pool was absorbed and the pump soon burned itself out.

The greatest problem for Enid was that the new Casa de Mastil staff was more interested in serving the paying guests than villa owners in residence. The owners didn't produce any income. When Enid in October faxed the hotel that she would occupy from January 20 to April 1 on the following year, a reply stated without apology that her dates were not available because the hotel was reserved for 22 weddings during that period. The hotel charged for everything from the minister to the bride's garter. As it turned out, few of the wedding party confirmed their initial room reservations at Casa de Mastil. Enid not only was denied the use of her villa but also lost the income from the supposed occupants that never showed up. Pedro was the only one that made money from the weddings.

Putting it all together Enid composed a letter of her need, regretfully, to sell La Arboleda. She cited increasing age and family problems as her reason for leaving Casa de Mastil.

16

Pedro looked at Enid's letter, reminded that he was the only one that could sell her property, IF he could sell it. He knew that he wasn't selling a title to a residence. He was only selling a piece of paper that alluded to the construction, the land below and his wife, Eugenia. This meant finding another Gringo that wanted to be on the ocean more than worry about the legal aspects of the deal. This meant that he would be losing a potential 50% down payment on a new villa in favor of a 10% agent's fee. He put the letter in the single file folder that held all his business papers.

He had more entrepreneurial projects to attend to, the first being another "partnership." This time it was with the farmer that was trying to grow corn in the sparse soil above Casa de Mastil. Pedro would supply the construction and the farmer would put up the land. Soon the corn crop was plowed under and the Mastil construction force hand mixed concrete for what looked like a floor slab for a new large house. On top of the concrete, the workers glued down something that looked like Astro Turf. No one could figure out his reason for the fake grass platform until a net was installed between two posts and white lines were painted in a rectangular pattern, Pedro had an answer for them. He had just created the first court in a complex to be called the Casa de Mastil Tennis Club and Cottages. He told guests that this would become the tennis center of Santa Rita. Yearly tournaments would bring in celebrities. Pedro added a thought.

"I could see an exhibition match with maybe Agassi and me against Courier and Jeff Woods."

A plan was posted in the hotel office that showed casitas strangely like those at Punta Viejo located on a hillside above the court. The new and only court in town attracted many of the locals. They soon learned that they were welcome to play on the new court providing that Pedro was included in the game. If they came without Pedro, a member of the hotel staff would announce that the court was not available. This wasn't entirely wrong, because the artificial surface kept coming unglued leaving ridges of turf that tripped up the players. Finally, even little children refused to play on such a mess, the net was removed and Pedro's court was closed down with a No Trespassing sign.

The botched Casa de Mastil Tennis Club was succeeded by an even more ambitious venture. In Steamboat Springs, Enid received a white 9 X 12 envelope. It was postmarked, El Paso. The return address was for a courier service that most Gringos in Mexico used to bring letters and packages across the border. This was faster and more reliable than the *Servicio Postal Mexicano*. Inside the envelope was a booklet with a large glossy color photo glued to its front page. It pictured a forty foot Bertram Sports Cruiser with a caption.

THE SANTA RITA YACHT CLUB

This is a special opportunity for Casa de Mastil owners and guests to invest in a lifetime of cruising and fishing pleasure. Under the experienced helm of Captain Alex McGovern, the SEA ROVER will take you directly from Casa de Mastil to the best Pacific fishing grounds to catch red snapper, sailfish, tarpon or the delicious mahi-mahi that abound just outside Santa Rita Bay. Captain McGovern will also take you whale watching, hunting for tortugas, our famous sea turtles, or to one of our remote beaches for a delightful day of gathering shells and picnicking.

MEMBERSHIP OPTIONS

COMMODORE. An initiation fee of USD $15,000 will allow you to reserve the SEA ROVER for a modest charge of USD $300 per day for 7 separate trips.

SKIPPER. For an initiation fee of USD $10,000, you may charter the boat for USD $500 per day for a total of 3 trips.

REGULATIONS. No smoking. No alcoholic beverages except as provided by the Captain. He shall be absolutely in charge during the entire trip. Appropriate dress shall be worn at all times. Tips and gratuities are not included in the prices.

EQUIPMENT. Captain McGovern will provide fishing gear and bait for fishing excursions. Club members should carry their own binoculars and sun-screen.

LIMITATIONS. In order to assure unlimited use of the boat at most times, membership shall be limited to 6 COMMODORES and 6 SKIPPERS.

Pedro was excited about a new venture that would give him something to counter with when neighbors in Punta Viejo discussed their Bohemian, Harvard or Union clubs. It was also a money-making scheme. He had learned that a Canadian skipper was looking for a winter operation to supplement his summer charters out of Victoria. In a series of phone conversations, McGovern was encouraged to bring the Bertram down to Mazatlan as the club's flagship. Pedro, as a 50% partner, agreed to put up $50,000 to purchase half of the SEA ROVER. He also assured McGovern that he would supply housing for his family and reimbursement for travel costs. McGovern would get 50% of all daily receipts, the remainder going to Casa de Mastil in return for making reservations and marketing. Pedro figured that he could get initiation fees for at least four of each membership category. He would pocket the balance after paying the $50,000 to McGovern.

The SEA ROVER arrived in Mazatlan but never left the dock. Those that might have joined would not have had any equity in Pedro's exclusive Yacht Club. They were already getting a 10% stock market return on the $10,000 or $15,000 that Pedro wanted for a membership. That could buy a lot of fishing trips. When Pedro saw that his scheme had failed, he denied that he'd ever guaranteed anything to Mc Govern. A sadder but enlightened skipper sailed the SEA ROVER back to Victoria.

Pedro looked for other income sources. Casa De Mastil had always provided some form of food service. In the early days short orders were prepared using Genie's kitchen in the Casa de Cabra. Later a palapa was built next to the bedrooms along the roadway where it would attract passersby. Pedro enthusiastically promoted the food service to a hotel guest.

"It's going to be wonderful. We will have lobsters and mahi-mahi. You can order a pizza from your villa by calling for room service!" The listener dropped a jaw in disbelief.

"How can we call for room service when there's no telephone?"

The lack of phones was not one of Pedro's cost-saving ideas. There were only four phones in all of Santa Rita. Two lines came into the hotel and a third the Santa Rita Café. All other calls in or out had to go thru a telephone located in a booth next to the ice cream store. Pedro had an answer.

"I have an idea. I will form a long tube out of hollow Bamboo and run it down the hillside. You can write your order, place it inside a small empty coconut and roll it down to the restaurant." He had no answer for how you got a return message.

Unfortunately, hotel guests compared his menus and his prices with the taco stands, palapas and bona-fide restaurants that made up the informal count of more than 30 eateries in Santa Rita. His guests seldom came back to the hotel for a second meal.

Pedro needed a way to coax diners back to his restaurant without spending any more money. He talked a chef named Francesco into signing a three year lease and constructing a pizza oven. Francesco was also to provide tables under two beautiful Bay trees on the ocean side of the roadway. The waterside dining attracted a new clientele until they found that their chairs sunk so far into the soft sand that some diners could hardly see over the tables.

Patronage at *Restaurante Mastil* increased to the point where Franceso needed a greeter and maitre'd. He interviewed a number of the potential candidates and his final choice was an Italian named Alberto, whose smiling greetings to everyone reflected skills acquired in his former life as a banker in Milan. The choice was good. Business increased even more as Alberto opened his arms to every woman that stepped near the restaurant. Without realizing how it would hurt his hotel income, Pedro knew he had a better role for Alberto. On each visit to the restaurant, Pedro talked about his great plans for new developments, additions to the hotel and his need to open a real estate office in the center of Santa Rita. He would need a good person to run that office.

Enid heard nothing from Pedro, or anyone else at the hotel, about prospective buyers for La Arboleda. After waiting two months without a report from him, Enid asked her friend, an attorney named Nancy Devereux, to help her write a letter to Pedro. It specifically asked how many times the property had been shown, whether it had been placed with local real estate offices, what marketing efforts were being made and whether the price she was asking seemed right. In answer to her demand for a response, Pedro finally called her to say,

"All of your concerns are being taken care of. You know that in Mexico property does not sell immediately, but the right buyer will come along."

"But Pedro, what about sales brochures and bringing in other agents?"

"I am preparing a color brochure that will be given to all the agents. It will be out in two weeks." Remembering his build-up to Alberto, he added, "As soon as I open the new real estate office in Santa Rita, a picture of La Arboleda will be featured on the walls."

"You have had an exclusive to sell my unit for almost a year, and haven't done any of the things you agreed to do to enhance a sale. You must be pushing your own units instead. You have a conflict of interest."

"I really don't like the….the inference, but, no, there is no possible conflict. I have a couple of other things to sell but they are smaller."

The idea that he was shading the truth never entered Pedro's mind. He had built a solid wall between his business and the moral world of right and wrong. Any sins in one area were forgiven in the other. The division became deeper as he strengthened his ties with the Evangelical movement. Each prayer session confirmed Pedro's belief that all of his works were good Christian undertakings that benefited the poor and the backward Santa Rita community. In fact, few of the workers at the hotel now came from Santa Rita. Housekeeper Maria was bringing in mothers and daughters from the remote hill towns who were happy to suffer long hours of trudging up the 152 steps with full buckets and mops and returning down with garbage and dirty linen. All this was in return for minimum wages that, he made complainers admit, were more money than they had ever seen before.

The Sessions also donated men and materials to build a small, supposedly nondenominational, chapel. It was built above his decaying tennis court where the casitas had been planned. In a town dominated by the Catholic Church for centuries, few shared his religion. The chapel suffered from the same low attendance rate as the tennis court, but it did serve honorably as a house of God for one Sunday a year. That was the week when doctors enlisted from the Sessions' church in Santa Monica donated their services. They freely diagnosed, prescribed, performed minor surgery and provided dental care to serve the poor and indigent of Santa Rita. They were housed for their stay in Casa de Mastil through the unoffered generosity of villa owners. Pedro provided this largess because a clause in the agreements allowed the hotel to use the villas for five nights a year for "Promotional purposes" One of the doctors was so impressed by Pedro's charitable zeal that he signed up for a yet-to-be built unit. The hotel was obviously headed in the correct, godly direction.

Pedro always looked for profit from his good works. Seeking more support for the hotel within Santa Rita, he donated $500 towards the construction of a new baseball park. This brought him an invitation from the Ejito leaders to attend the opening ceremonies. They asked him to be the honorary catcher for the first pitch. A proud Pedro stepped behind the plate and raised a new mitt in anticipation of the first delivery. That pitch whistled through his opened hands and grazed an ear. Pedro winced and rubbed the bruise as the townspeople in the stands cheered.

He had not been told that the Honorary Pitcher was an angry next door neighbor that lived downstream from the hotel's inadequate sewer system. The neighbor was a victim caught between Pedro's requirement to build a new sewer line and the village's failure to repair an obsolete waste treatment plant at the end of the line. Pedro's immediate solution was to stop his pipe and dump the effluent into a concrete tank. The tank that overflowed into the roadway and stank up the neighborhood had been built right in front of the neighbor's house.

Enid returned to Steamboat to enjoy the summer days. There, she got one short call from Pedro to say that he had a great prospective buyer in the US. It was someone that wanted to trade a bed and breakfast located in a remote town near Silverton, Colorado for her unit at Casa de Mastil. Enid laughed at Pedro's proposal. All she needed was another cold-weather mountain property!

She enjoyed the great July and August weather that pulled city dwellers to the Rockies. It ended too quickly. The highest peaks in the distant Flat Tops became splashed with white from the first snowfall. One day there was full foliage and the next bare branches as the Western Slope jumped into sunless, doldrums-like days. Santa Rita had its own problems with the forces of nature. In late September, a small storm started off the coast near Acapulco and gained momentum as it suddenly veered north. The threat of high winds in Mazatlan was usually remote and seldom worried residents. Most hurricanes stayed south of Manzanillo, but this storm continued to head up the coast and soon was rated a number 3 hurricane. As it hit the city of Puerto Vallarta it wiped out great chunks of the Malecon, overturned yachts in the Marina and sent tourists quickly inland. Worried Casa de Mastil owners called and sent faxes to Pedro, asking if there were damages to their units.

Pedro saw a chance for a self-serving gain from the storm. In an unusual, written communication to all owners Pedro described the horrors. The Sessions had hidden in their Bodega for hours while wind-blown trees and palapa roofs bounced overhead. He included a paragraph about how staff homes had been destroyed or at the least severely damaged. His concluding paragraph stated:

"It is too soon to estimate the extent of damage from such a terrible storm, but to cover immediate costs I ask each of you to send me a check for $1,000."

Curious, Enid called her friend Nancy Devereux who was still in Santa Rita, to find out what could be done to help those hurt by the hurricane. Much to her surprise Nancy was very calm and hardly upset as she said,

"Santa Rita was lucky. The eye traveled due North with circling winds at the edges. The worst gusts were softened by the mountains that surround the town. There were a few flying palm fronds and a few damaged palapas. As far as I know Casa de Mastil was doubly protected by the point and should have had no damage." Enid did not respond to Pedro's impassioned request. She saw only that this man had cheated her from the beginning, had lied to her consistently and now was committing what she was sure was a fraud.

17

Enid spent the month of November traveling in India with her friend Nancy Devereux. There, during a delay in flight between Delhi and Bombay, they again discussed the terms of Enid's original purchase contract. Nancy agreed with Enid that Pedro was at least dishonest and possibly a crook. Although he himself was tight-lipped, his different shady schemes had become common gossip. For Enid he had failed to live up to his end of the contract or follow through with his subsequent written assurances to market the villa. It was obvious that his main interest in La Arboleda was to use it to show prospects his design and construction abilities. Enid soon caught on to his methods. He would first call, announcing that he had a prospective buyer for Enid's villa. When the party arrived, Enid noticed that Pedro extolled the beauty of La Arboleda but never suggested it was for sale. After their visit he would take the prospects to another site and glowingly describe how he could build a unit with all of the same quality features and sell it to them for a lesser price.

"Oh, yes," he said, "she told me she wanted to sell; but I refused to help her because of the exorbitant asking price."

Enid learned more about Pedro who was now an adversary. His architectural education was limited to a one semester review course and his stay at the New York Studio School was aborted by his father. She could picture him as a troubled youth making his first trip to Santa Rita to avoid the draft. Now, that didn't seem like such a big crime after all. As she watched him head to the beach on the few days that he came back to Santa Rita, she saw that the ocean had become both his sanctuary and a corollary for his social attitudes. There were good waves and bad waves. He was probably never sure of the difference until he rode one. A bad wave was soon forgotten as he paddled back to the break point and tried again. A bad deal was similarly forgotten. A new wave, a new deal, was due to come sometime soon. She saw that Pedro, Peter Oliver Sessions, had developed his own code of ethics and his own counsel for success. The tricks she heard about in tennis allowed him to compete with those stronger or more agile. Tricks in making money followed suit. He would never get advice from others to avoid making mistakes. There was no one to help him decide which wave to take or what deal to make.

Pedro, himself, didn't dwell on his business traits and usually ascribed any of his social problems to his reserve and natural shyness. He knew that he had trouble communicating about anything with anyone; but excused this as part of his artistic makeup. His building designs were original in their approach and his arrogance was only to protect their integrity. Pedro seemed to be confusing originality with brilliance and artistic license with just bad ideas. When it came to business dealings, Pedro admitted that he enjoyed the sense of control that came with the design of a building and looked for the same satisfaction from his financial schemes. Moreover, he wanted to become part of the competitive world where entrepreneurs tried to best each other with bigger homes, bigger jets and bigger social events.

He wanted to be known, as if that might compensate for the loneliness common to one so within himself. It was all part of surfing through life. He was being gathered up by these new energy forces and would soon command the crest, maybe having to lean a little to the legal left or right to stay on his course. This was not hard in a remote Mexican village where donations to local officials—graft grants—were the accepted way to meet the foolish regulations that some beaurocrat in Mexico City had set up. Everyone was doing it.

Pedro finally opened the promised real estate office in the village. A simple painted sign on the wall of a former furniture shop announced the name of Santa Rita Realty. Little had been done inside the building beyond providing an office desk and chairs for an agent and a prospective buyer. To operate it, Pedro sweet-talked Alberto into becoming the sales manager with promises of great opportunities to use his natural talents. Enid was Alberto's first visitor in the new office. She hoped that he would put a greater effort into selling her property than Pedro had. Her hope faded when she saw a picture of La Arboleda hung on the wall between two other villas. There was no indication near the picture, or anywhere else in the office, that the villa was available. The brochures that Pedro had promised months before were non-existent. As she discussed the potential sale with Alberto, even offering him a bonus beyond the 10% agent's fee, he smilingly assured her that he wanted to sell her villa but told her,

"When I asked Pedro for information about the size, sale price and the purchase agreement, he just answered, 'You just find the customers and bring them to me. I will make the deal.'"

In hopes of accelerating his own sales, Pedro invented more attractions to tempt potential buyers. He advertised that a new Jetta Station Wagon was available for the convenience of renters. The wagon was seldom available because it was taking their son to school or Genie to visit friends around Punta Viento. Pedro then convinced a local van driver to paint *Casa de Mastil Taxi* on the front doors of the vehicle. Guests making reservations were introduced to the new service with a note in their confirmation package.

The spirit of Casa de Mastil starts with an escort waiting at the airport arrival gate. Your guide, experienced with the local lore and history, will provide you with direct transportation to Santa Rita in our exclusive passenger van.

Guests soon found that the $100.00 ride from the airport cost twice that in any other cab.

Enid found more faults with her villa as she waited for some action towards its sale. The expensive jet system in her pool failed. The pumps and the pool heater were located in the *bodega* below Enid that the hotel used for temporary storage. There was so much bedding and furniture crammed into the space that it was impossible for maintenance people to service the pool equipment. The bedding also caused a near disaster. One of the staff had stuffed a mattress up against a light bulb. In the middle of the night Enid awoke to smoke fumes. She saw flames lapping up to her deck from the fire below. She called the night watchman, but of course the office was locked up so he could not answer the phone. In her nightgown she rushed down to the bodega, pulled the burning mass out of the bodega, and wrestled it into one of Pedro's otherwise useless troughs that he'd made to catch the overflow from her pool.

Enid tried hand-delivered and faxed appeals to both Pedro and Genie, demanding that they fulfill their obligations or re-consider the clauses in the contract relating to the sale. She asked how they could justify 10% when they were not doing any of the things that normal realtors did to market a residence. How could they justify an exclusive right to sell? When Pedro finally relented and offered a partial fee to other brokers, Enid went to discuss the sale with Alveras Realty, one of the oldest brokers in the area. She asked the agent,

"Would you take on the sales of my villa?" The broker smiled in response.

"No one will do that here. We all had experiences with Pedro that were distasteful."

"Such as?"

"Such as not sharing the agent's fee. Such as being close to making a sale and having Eugenia refuse to sign over the Presta Nombre. Such as a real question about the validity of his agreements. He has been faking the sale to foreigners of Ejito land that he has no right to sell and they have no right to buy. Come back when the property has been Regularized and you have a clear title to sell. Then we can make a deal."

"Regularizing? What does that mean?" Enid asked. In response, the broker covered the history of land ownership in Santa Rita. He told her about the Restricted Zone within 50 kilometers of the ocean where foreigners were not allowed to buy property. He reminded her that Santa Rita was Ejito land, owned in common by the Mexicans. The Ejito council could sell parcels to Mexicans and the Mexicans could resell to foreigners when the government had freed the land through a process called Regularization. Enid was dumbstruck. Her contract with Pedro was useless.

"Is there any way to make my property saleable?"

The agent explained that even though Mexicans legally owned the land, it was illegal for them to sell to Gringos with the name-lending device called a Presta Nombre. The Presta Nombre ruse was against every law; but the federal government was anxious to encourage more Norte Americanos to bring their dollars to Mexico, particularly along the tourist-attracting coastlines. Therefore they passed a law saying that, when the land was Regularized, foreigners could hold indirect title by having it put into a trust with a Mexican bank naming the foreigner as a beneficiary.

"When will all this be possible?"

"None of us know. The Regularization has been piecemeal, often cutting a piece of property in half so that the owner still can't sell it. The government has been swamped with requests for Regularization. When? Remember that you are in Mexico!"

Enid realized that, although her contract with the Sessions inferred—by their demand for exclusive agency—that they had given her the rights to use the land, it would never be saleable until the hotel land was Regularized. The present contract would never be given credence by a Mexican judge. She'd just have to wait.

Back at her villa, Enid forgot her real estate problems as she walked into her kitchen. Fruits were scattered over the floor. A banana was half eaten. An avocado skin lay beside it. The peanuts had disappeared from a snack food bowl. When she finally found someone to help, they smiled and said,

"You have been raided by a *Tlacuache.*"

In her book on Mexican flora and fauna she found that this was a creature with the look of a bristled sloth but the canniness of a Raccoon. The Tlacuache had come in through the open end of the living area. Even foods carefully stored in plastic boxes were stolen. The animal seemed like an appropriate mascot for the hotel.

Next, she looked towards the ocean and was surprised to see that two deck chairs with fading canvas seats had been placed near the pool. A note was pinned to one saying that these were on loan from Pedro but could be purchased for $700 apiece. She noticed the number 545 stenciled on one of the wood frames. She realized that they were chairs from a distressed sale, probably from one of the tour boats. She thought that she could do much better than pay $700 for second hand chairs. She had seen some at an umbrella rental casita on the beach. The umbrella man thought she could find them in the village of El Cajon. There she drove up and down the streets of the small town looking for deck chairs. Finally she stopped at a small furniture store to ask about *Silla de la Playa.* A salesman told her,

"We can get them for you very soon. They are made in my hometown near Guadalajara. How many do you want, Senora?"

"How much? Quanta cuesta?"

"Oh, for around 160 pesos each, I think."

"Will you guarantee?"

"Of course, Senora."

Enid ordered half a dozen deck chairs, thrilled that she had been lucky enough to find the source.
Two weeks later she was aroused at one o'clock Sunday morning by a rattle of her gate.

"Senora Williams? It is I with your chairs. I am sorry. My truck broke down. I will bring them to you now."

"Where is your truck? Can't you come back tomorrow?"

"It is in Santa Rita pueblo being fixed. Tomorrow is not possible. I will not have the truck then."

The man and a friend climbed up the 152 steps carrying the six chairs on their heads.

"But I thought they would all have the green fabric we agreed on!"

"I am sorry Senora, this is all there is." Each chair had a different fabric and all of them had unfinished wood parts, some already splintered. "I have done my best to fill your order."

Given the hour, Enid paid him for the chairs whose price had increased to 180 pesos.
Falling back asleep she spoke to the empty room,

"Oh well, I've saved over six hundred dollars a chair!"

Enjoying the good things about Santa Rita, Casa de Mastil and La Arboleda could lighten Enid's despair over not selling the villa, or more properly not being able to sell her contract with Genie as the Presta Nombre. She now accepted another reason why Pedro wasn't making any effort to sell her villa. He legally had nothing to sell. She had no idea when Regularization might take place and wondered if she could sue him for his lack of performance. She had heard about an English speaking lawyer that was close to the political scene in Tepic. Looking for some kind of help, she faxed a long list of questions to the woman:

8.   Here is a copy of our agreement in English and Spanish. Is it valid under Mexican law?

9.   Can I as a non-citizen sue for the Sessions' failure to perform under the terms of their contract?

10.   Is there a law against conflicts of interest?

11.   If I sell, will agreement terms pass on to new buyer?

12.   Is it possible to have property "Regularized" without Sessions' consent?

In an exchange of mixed messages, it finally turned out that the woman wasn't a lawyer. She was *a contador* or accountant, but her father was the *abogado*. Unfortunately the father couldn't speak more than three words of English and Enid dropped the search.

Next she heard about Cornell Davis, a North American who was practicing law in Mexico. After he received a $500 retainer fee, he started to research the terms of the Williams/Sessions agreement. The first thing he reported to Enid was that she had been deceived by Pedro's agreement to supply her with a Spanish version prepared by a *Notario Publico*. Even though the document was properly written in Spanish, the notary's stamp only verified a statement of the interpreter that he had made an accurate translation. The Notario took no responsibility for its content. Enid wanted Davis to determine possible ways to force Peter Oliver and Isabella Eugenia Sessions to sell the rights to "her" property. After a month Enid requested a progress report and was told that they were very close to an answer. After a second month she was told that they had been investigating the wrong property.

18

Former Santa Ritans Rusty and Juan were standing together near one of the useless settling ponds of the village's defunct sewer plant. The remains of the plant were located on an hectare of flat land near where the river flowed into the Pacific. Rusty had returned to Santa Rita during a lull in American homebuilding and was looking forward to once again enjoy the great surfing. Juan was there to follow up a tip on a possible land deal. The two former beach bums had unexpectedly run into each other the evening before and had spent most of the night in a celebratory reunion. Since the last time they met, they had matured respectively into a successful real estate broker and a wealthy businessman. Rusty was dressed in polo shirt and khakis and Juan had on a bright yellow shirt tucked into designer jeans. Two other men that might once have been boxers stood at a discreet distance from the two friends. The muscle men were dressed in white tee shirts left loose to hang over black polyester pants.

On the previous night Rusty and Juan exchanged memories of the past. When the subject of Pedro came up, Juan described the rumors he'd heard about how Pedro had stolen La Casa de Cabra. Rusty shrugged off his loss as if cheating was just part of the real estate game. Now they paced along what they thought were the boundaries of the treatment plant. In front of them a concrete bunker with weather stained walls stood as a reminder of the once operating system. Three horses were feeding on grass along the riverbank. A row of palm trees marked the division between the site and a long stretch of white beach sand with the ocean beyond. The rest of the land held nothing but brown and burned grass. Rusty spoke first,

"What do you think, Amigo?"

"Get rid of the shit and we have the greatest site on the coast for a new hotel!"

"How? How do we move the treatment plant?"

"I have friends."

Since his last stay in Santa Rita, Juan had grown from mule to major player in the delicate business of distributing recreational drugs. His operation was enhanced when he inherited his family's chain of mom and pop stores, each with a different name but all under the same ownership. The small shops throughout Mexico provided a perfect cover for his operations. Each shopkeeper was a distributor. In the rear of each shop an Apple Macintosh relayed drug orders and sales records on the new Internet to Juan's headquarters. Juan kept a tight lip about his activities, but as they talked Rusty could predict something not quite legal based upon Juan's history. After saying that he would contact Rusty as soon as he had more information, Juan shook his hand, said goodbye, and left followed by his two *guardaespaldas* two steps behind.

Two days later Juan was sitting in an Equipale chair at a table in Las Olas restaurant. Instead of his usual bodyguards, he was joined for lunch by a Bikini-clad Meztisos half his age. They both picked at full plates of fish ceviche, each anticipating with different feelings the inevitable next move to his room above. The reverie was interrupted when a local real estate agent walked through the open gate of the restaurant and paused beside the pots of bougainvillea. Spotting Juan the agent walked to his table.

"Buenos tardes, Señor. It is so grand to see you and to meet your lovely wife. I have been looking all over for you. I have good news." Juan was not pleased to be interrupted at such a delicate moment but knew he must recognize the real estate agent and replied,

"I would like you to meet.......Juanita. What is your good news?"

"I have made an arrangement with the Ejito concerning your desire to take over the sewer treatment plant. They understand that as the new land owner you are committed to improve the system for the good of the community that you love."

"And then what?"

"I have found an engineer with a new system that takes little space and is not at great cost. He tells me that his treatment machine can be located anywhere along the river. There is much empty land upstream where you could move the treatment plant."

"Let us talk more in your office at five o'clock tonight. Thank you for your visit." He waved the agent away.

Late that afternoon Juan found Rusty and, followed by Juan's two constant associates, they entered Alveras Realty. While the bodyguards remained in the foyer to read the well-fingered magazines on a coffee table, the partners went into a back office. There the agent gave Rusty and Juan more details about the proposed transactions. He said that the Ejido was anxious to sell off any land they could in order to pay for improvements in the Santa Rita road and water systems.

A *Notario Publico* prepared a purchase agreement that was signed by the new partners and the members of the Ejito council. The agreement transferred the property to what Juan named the Pacific Land Development Corporation in return for an improved sanitary system. The sale became public knowledge. When the local citizenry criticized the village fathers for the sale, they defended the plan, claiming that the beachside site would inevitably be developed at some time anyway. The fathers knew that questions about the land sale would die down. It was not as important an issue at present as the condition of the rutted, muddy roads and the limited water supply. Sewage treatment was a secondary concern for the average villager. The question of where it all went was forgotten as soon as a toilet was flushed.

Across town Pedro Sessions was courting a new prospect as they put away surfboards they'd been using for much of the afternoon. Pedro and Grant England had met the previous year on the beach where they exchanged ideas about the ocean waves breaking before them. Grant was one of the hundreds of surfers who continually looked for a new beach, a new wave pattern, and a new challenge. When Pedro invited him to return and stay at Casa de Mastil Grant quickly accepted. At Casa Mastil, Grant and his wife were being treated by the Sessions to the hospitality that they reserved for prospective buyers. Each day Genie drove them on a different tour around Santa Rita. Each night they were treated to seafood meals in a variety of restaurants.

They were impressed by Pedro's description of how he had built up the hotel from nothing. They were also pleased to learn of the faith of this serious, God-loving Samaritan. At an appropriate time, Pedro introduced an idea. He told Grant that a large piece of property adjacent to Casa de Mastil was possibly for sale. He said that the terms seemed so good that the Sessions were thinking of buying it in order to keep the tree-filled open space as a buffer to the hotel. He asked Grant,

"Would you be interested in participating in the purchase as a long-term investment? I am sure that every dollar invested here will yield at least two within five years. We had planned to buy the lot on our own but we would like to share such a good deal with friends."

Grant had land in Oregon whose stand of Douglas firs had reached merchantable status and he was anxious to sell. Casa de Mastil looked like a great place to reinvest the money and when he said so to Pedro the two contacted the owner of the property next door. They negotiated a purchase of the oceanfront property by pledging Grant's land in Oregon as a first payment with the balance due in a year. The seller agreed that, should there be any unpaid balance after that, it would be treated as a loan with favorable interest rates. There was a drawback. The seller insisted on dealing with only one principal.

Pedro reluctantly agreed that Grant could be the lead and that he, Pedro, would contribute his half of the purchase price. The timber piece was soon traded. When it came time for Pedro to put up his share of the deal, he suggested a different plan to Grant.

"I think it would be nice to expand Casa de Mastil. The new villas could be built on our jointly-owned land and still leave plenty of open space as a buffer. We could set up a corporation. You provide the land. I will design and construct the villas. We will sell the villas and share the profits fifty-fifty"

Grant thought about possible pitfalls, but soon agreed because of the quick return that Pedro assured him on his investment. Grant soon found that he might have jumped too quickly. Pedro claimed that, as a 50% partner, Grant had to pay his share of the costs to prepare the Articles of Incorporation of the new Santa Rita Development Corporation. Grant had thought that was Pedro's responsibility as the developer. He reluctantly put up the amount that Pedro said was his 50% share. It actually covered the entire cost.

The England and Sessions property lay just west of La Arboleda and the sculptural Casa de Mastil stairway. Its treed valley was ringed on the south and west by a steep hill that became a rock cliff face as it reached towards the ocean. The cliff face stood out as a natural landmark that could be seen from any point on the crescent shaped beach. Pedro, as usual, didn't disclose his plans to anyone, so Enid was surprised by and curious about a cobbled stone road that was being built up the edge of the valley to connect with the public way just above Enid's villa. She thought all the land beyond the stairs was simply jungle, perhaps controlled by the government. Then she saw land to the east of the new road leveled and covered with sod grass. She suspected this was Pedro's work when she watched men install a putting green covered with Astroturf that had to have been salvaged from the abandoned tennis court.

Enid finally picked up the rumors about Pedro's deal with a new patsy called Grant England. The area that the two had purchased dominated Enid's foreground view. Unattractive buildings in her view corridor would make her property even harder to sell when, and if, the Regularization took place. She confronted Pedro on one of his few visits to Santa Rita and asked him to describe his ideas for the land. He replied,

"I want to create a beautiful area for unforgettable weddings. Most of the space will become a grassed platform for the ceremonies and guest seating. I might place a few villas on top of the roadway. They will be called Las Villas con Corazon, the villas of the heart. As the roadway passes underneath it will become the Tunnel of Love."

"How nice." Enid's sarcasm was lost on Pedro. She thought,

"At least, he didn't use that name on my villa."

In March, Grant returned to Mexico to check on Pedro's progress. He first looked over the corporation books. As promised, Pedro had put some pesos into the corporation account but had then withdrawn them as a "Real Estate Agent's Fee." Grant hoped to see villas constructed on the property that echoed the designs of Las palmas or La Arboleda, but Pedro had only built the new road and what Grant would learn was called The Kissing Lawn. Grant noticed that some workers were chipping away a small section of the rock face of the landmark cliff. He found Pedro as he came down the steps from Enid's and asked for a report on what was happening. Pedro told him,

"They are making the ground level and trimming out loose rocks. This is the location for the first of the villas. It will be called *Pacifico.*"

Grant then set up a formal meeting time with Pedro in order to review all the plans. He never got to see them because the meeting was cancelled. Pedro suddenly was called for an "important conference in Guadalajara." Grant spent the time reviewing the corporation books that Pedro had given him the day before. He didn't like what he saw. He asked himself why Pedro took out as operating costs whatever he put in as a capital contribution. How were they going to pay the balance due on the sale? Grant was annoyed with Pedro's absence when he wanted to talk to him. Distraught, Grant returned to Oregon and reviewed his position. He realized that he would never be a true partner in the deal and E-mailed Pedro that he wanted to withdraw and that he expected prompt repayment of his investment in the land.

Pedro E-mailed back his sincere regrets, noting how difficult it was for him to have Grant go back on his word. He then suggested that, in lieu of repaying Grant for relinquishing his share of the partnership, Pedro would build him a villa. He offered a one-story 2-bedroom villa over the Tunnel of Love. In an exchange of E-mails, different options were discussed. Pedro finally conceded that a 3-bedroom unit could be built on the very top of the cliff. Grant would be able to drive right to it on an easement that Pedro claimed he owned along the hilltop.

In June a prominent landmark was about to disappear. The operation was purposely planned during the summer when most Norte Americanos had returned to the states. They missed the sight of Pedro bringing in two dozen men and a D-7 Caterpillar tractor. The men's pickaxes and shovels slowly ate away the cliff at the end of the beach and the tractor dumped the material along the shoreline. Gradually the human jackhammers began consuming the very land that Pedro had designated for Grant England's villa.

The damage to one of the town's important natural features could be seen by anyone that walked along the beach. Finally, the operations prompted local officials to warn him that he must have all the necessary permits. They cautioned him that the state and the nation were getting more careful about providing open space and preserving trees in the jungle lands. Where was his Environmental Assessment Report? Pedro professed innocence, saying that he'd built the best project in Santa Rita and didn't know he needed such a report. He described his removal of the cliff as a safety measure to remove loose rock and then said to the officials,

"As you can see, I have preserved all of the beautiful trees. Why can't I get the report now?" When gratuities were handed out, the officials suggested a plan. If Pedro would get a map of all the remaining trees as required for an Environmental Assessment, they could backdate it and that should permit him to finish what they described as "Exploratory Excavation." Pedro hired a surveyor to mark and catalogue all the trees at Casa de Mastil. The officials imposed a token penalty for Pedro's laxity by temporarily closing down one of his units. Bands of yellow tape and signs forbidding entry were placed around one of the villas. The selected property was Enid's La Aborleda!

When Enid found the entrance to her villa blocked she rushed down to the front office and demanded that they remove the tape.

"Senora Williams, this is just a momentary nuisance. The tapes will be removed shortly," she was told.

"But why are they there?"

"There has been a mix-up about permits for the new work. It is being resolved now"

"What does my villa have to do with the new work?"

"There seems to be some question about past permits. Your villa was the easiest to seal off. As I say, it is all being resolved."

"I will not suffer for Pedro's past problems. I am going to take down the tapes myself!"

The desk clerk shrugged his shoulders as she turned and walked away. Enid was angry and became more so, as she realized that the undisturbed view that Pedro had promised her was changing. She watched in horror as the men gradually cut into the stone face and the tractor started filling what had been tideland. She spoke out loud to the vista.

"What the Hell's going on? Do you think this is Mount Rushmore? Are you going to carve in the head of El Presidente?"

She, of course, wasn't heard as the men, working in shifts throughout the day-light hours, cut at the cliff and the Cat removed the spoils. They removed the soft rock to set the cliff back over 25 meters. The spoils that were dumped along the edge of the beach created a "Lido" for the hotel that illegally invaded the Federal Coastal Zone. This strip above the mean high tide line was supposedly protected against all environmental changes and was always open to public use. The most prominent natural features of Bahia Santa Rita had been summarily defaced and the Federal Zone violated. One thing was obvious. There would be no Tunnel of Love.

Having complied with the official requests that he have an Environmental Assessment, Pedro then was free to apply for a bona fide planning permit for the new property. His application described a total of eight residences to be built "in a manner similar to the existing villas." By definition, a residence was no more than two stories tall. He guessed that he could tweak those figures as the work progressed. He had only temporary qualms about skirting a law that had never been in play in Santa Rita. He deeply believed that any restraint on his development was limiting business that benefited his community. He had used that business to employ villagers and used proceeds from the business to build a church and help a baseball team. In his mind, these were big things for Santa Rita.

His confusing mixture of compulsive ambition, religious zeal, real estate profits and civic contributions always put a strain on the hotel operation. Now there emerged a new side of Pedro: an autocratic demand for total allegiance from his staff. He, not an employee, was the one to make every decision, no matter how small. He began to dictate the number of rolls of toilet paper to be left in each room, the frequency of linen changes, even the menu for the restaurant. In a business where service meant everything, he was stifling the initiatives of employees that needed to make on the spot decisions to keep guests happy. If he occasionally thought that he might be hurting his employees, he remembered his preacher's proclamation.

"Every time we sin, we crucify Christ anew! By taking Christ into your heart, it is he that absorbs the pain."

Pedro did not admit there were many sins. He was convinced that not following local *mordisco* traditions of paying government officials under the table would be an insult to the Mexicans he dealt with. He was sure that if this was committing a sin, his guilt would be lifted as it wended its way to Christ. His Lord had a lot of experience in accepting burdens.

Pedro's encounter with the laws about environmental conservation produced a momentary epiphany. He became a conservationist. Pedro had all along planned to build the equivalent of an apartment building where he had cut away the cliff. In his usual practice of keeping his ideas to himself, not even Manuel knew about the concept. Now Pedro had found a commendable reason for his plan. Before, he had always taken the jungle for granted. Trees were trees. Flowers were for table decorations. He did not understand the critical relationships within an eco-system; but his concept would count as preserving the natural environment. He could claim to have saved dozens of trees and plants by concentrating all of his proposed units in one place. If that one place was where he'd cut away the rocky cliff, he wouldn't destroy anything green. It was only incidental that this location would have the best views in Casa de Mastil.

He began to implement his new concept. Instead of the permitted eight buildings spread out along the flat, he would stack the eight buildings on top of each other. Normally, such a large building would have an architect prepare plans to coordinate spaces and infrastructure. Pedro's best design ideas came to him when he could see some bare-bones structure in place. He didn't want an architect to take this away from him. If he could see a bunch of open floors, he could work his magic cutting the space into units and placing walls where he wanted them. Pedro hired an engineer to figure column and beam sizes for a structure that looked like a parking garage. He purchased a small electric concrete mixer and Manuel began to construct columns on the engineer's recommended spacing of three meters. He used six by six posts to support wooden formwork and long steel reinforcing rods to make beams and slabs for a floor above. It was like stacking upside-down tables on top of each other. This was repeated for floors two, three, four and five.

Each step that Manuel took produced a disaster in waiting. The mixer was so small that concrete had to be poured in layers. There were no vibrators to blend the layers together and, when the concrete was dropped into the column forms, the ingredients separated, destroying the necessary bond. No one had told him that this was a seismic zone and his type of construction was the first to fail in an earthquake. The weakest point was where the posts met the slabs. If Pedro had looked under any table, he would have seen that there was always extra reinforcing where the legs met the tops. Pedro was never that curious.

Although it was unfinished, Pedro found new, would-be buyers to pay to turn this skeleton into habitable space. They failed at this stage to realize that there was no elevator. Each floor had to be reached by steep stairways. The corridors that ran along the back of the structure were very long and terminated in dead ends that provided only one exit in case of fire or other emergencies.

In November a colored architectural rendering appeared on a sign near the river in Santa Rita. It announced that a new hotel would be constructed by the Pacific Development Corporation on the beach. Although the site was not specifically described, most of the locals knew by now that a deal had been made between the Ejito Board and two former residents. The rendering didn't show that Juan and Rusty had commissioned architectural drawings for a 6 story building. Although every other structure along the beach was only two stories high, Juan had found a dusty copy of the county zoning code that allowed a string of 6 story buildings along the waterfront. Few in Santa Rita had ever worried about a code, or even knew of its existence, because most of the village land belonged to the Ejito. The details of the new hotel meant little to most of the townspeople who were pleased that the developers had already purchased a small lot upstream and authorized construction of a new sewage treatment system. The timing was apt because an unusual December storm had flooded the riverside lands and destroyed most of the settling beds. Although kept secret from the tourists, the effluent from the useless plant was now flowing directly into the sea.

19

Grant England drove the road to Santa Rita with an anticipation that he hadn't felt since the days driving with his parents to the beach at Seaside. Although often plagued by Oregon's fog, visiting Seaside's long stretch of sand and crashing Pacific waves meant a time of freedom from his school regime and household chores. Now on Mexico Highway 200 he had similar expectations and this time it included his first view of his new villa at Casa de Mastil. Pedro had glowingly described it in faxes and e-mails.

"Commanding hilltop location! Sweeping ocean views through a row of arches! Brick boveda domes and a huge palapa over the living area."

Grant envisioned Pedro's deft touch, applying the best details of Enid Williams' villa to his own that would sit on the brow of the hill with ocean views in three directions. He hardly noticed any of the plastic and metal refuse that was a growing patina over Mexico's resort landscape. The travel route was familiar to him. He drove along the cobbled entrance road, across the bridge and down Independencia. The streets hadn't lost their dust and dogs but he was amazed by the amount of new, and what he thought was not very appealing, construction. There was no homage paid to old Mexican towns where street fronts formed a continuous wall. Even La Barraca, the oldest building in town, had been rudely modernized by adding a fifth story. He made a right turn and then drove along the beach road until it reached the Casa de Mastil entrance. He glanced at the planted ship's prow that announced arrival into a special place and then braked the car to a sudden halt. He looked to the top of the ridge above the hotel, exclaiming,

"The Bastard! He's cut down my cliff! He's destroyed my homesite!"

Grant proceeded along the public road whose former dirt path had been replaced by colored concrete, patterned to look like brick paving. He could see that Pedro had, in effect, turned the historic public route to the cemetery and beach into what felt like a private terrace. The old roadside rooms scrapped from a garage had been remodeled again into waterside *casitas*!

Grant stopped the car in disbelief. Directly in front of him was an open wall of concrete posts and floor slabs. It stretched across the entire face of what had been the cliff and, he counted, the formwork was five levels high. It stopped just short of the ridge cut that had caused him to brake his car.

Approaching the new behemoth, he found a smiling Manuel directing the installation of formwork for what appeared to be level six of the tower.

"¿Que pasa, Manuel? ¿Que Pasa?"

"Esta Mi Departamento de Playa! ¿ Es bonito? ¿ Si?"

The foreign population of Santa Rita was expanding with an influx of Southern Coloradans that wanted to escape the cold. They were joined by California super-surfers seeking ever-greater wave-induced thrills. The new residents had purchased second homes in the quiet fishing village because they liked its unspoiled ambience: the boats lined up on the beach, the modest but brightly colored buildings, a village contained by the tree-covered hills that embraced the town. Each new arrival expected Santa Rita to remain the place that they'd first discovered. The Californians called it a rustic Carmel, the Coloradans a seaside Aspen. None of the foreigners stopped to think that such picturesque towns were kept that way by rigid planning and zoning codes so the Gringos, joined by expatriates from Mexico City, were in disbelief that the "high-rise" under construction at the west end could actually be built next to their beach. They next assumed that further floors might be halted by the authorities and finally asked whether there actually were controls to limit such overbuilding in Santa Rita. Pedro's new construction at Casa de Mastil became a rallying point for their concerns. What could be done?

Nancy Devereux had gone to Harvard Law School with a Mexican attorney named Doctor Ernesto Chavez. He was a lawyer, but in Mexico professionals were accorded the same title as medical physicians. Dr. Chavez had a practice that specialized in the control of growth along the seacoasts of the world. Nancy suggested to Enid that they might invite Ernesto to make a social visit to Santa Rita in the hopes that he might recognize the threats of unwelcome growth and agree to help control them.

A taxi dropped Ernesto off on the beach road not far from Casa de Castil. He stroked his short mustache and ran a hand over his dark hair that had been wind-blown during the taxi ride. A rust colored wall along the road's edge was broken by a plaster archway with its wrought iron gate. He pushed through the gate and started to climb towards the villa above. The concrete steps were broken up by landings and each landing had fanciful beach stone inlays of sea fish or creeping Iguanas. At the top of the steps a wide, carved wooden door was opened by a man whose white, starched jacket looked unusual as it sat uneasily above a pair of badly wrinkled khaki shorts.

"Senor…Doctore Chavez?"

"Si."

"Por favor, la sala a la derecha." The part-time houseman pointed him to the room on his right. He entered a living area whose high ceilings were accented by rows of dark-stained beams. A cocktail party in his honor was in session. He walked across a floor of waxed tile towards the French doors that opened the entire room to a large terrace. At the doors he was greeted by Nancy. He was introduced to many of the guests and finally left to chat with Enid. When the name of Sessions was mentioned, he said that he was very familiar with their history. As a teacher he had used Santa Rita to study what would happen if the existing zoning was allowed to remain as written for this Mexican coastal town. This was the first time that Enid had heard that Santa Rita actually had zoning.

Almost three years had passed from the day that she had notified the Sessions of her intent to sell La Arboleda. Despite her anger with the Sessions, she had become philosophical about using her villa whenever possible and participating more in community affairs. She knew from local realtors that there was no way she could sell until the land was Regularized. Wryly remembering one of Doug's jokes, she told herself,

"If you're going to be screwed you might as well lie back and enjoy it."

Towards the end of the party she talked again with Dr. Chavez and asked him if he might help her resolve her problems with Pedro. Dr. Chavez seemed intrigued, especially if it involved the Sessions and the chance to stop their unbridled development. The next day he met Enid at La Arboleda and as they talked

Enid realized that there was a bigger issue than selling her villa. Chavez told her how the Mexican government was pushing for massive development along both coasts in order to promote tourism. They had tried to force a dozen high-rise hotels upon a village south of Puerto Vallarta that was similar to Santa Rita until he helped the town successfully combat the plan.

Chavez suggested that if a group of locals formed and legally incorporated an association, they would then have an official voice. The association could then be represented at the many government levels to stop the overdevelopment of Santa Rita. Chavez said that he knew the government officials were being paid off by Pedro and that an investigation of all the facts might stop the tower construction, bring closure to Pedro's illegal moves and force him to accept Regularization of Casa de Mastil.

Chavez described how to form an activist group. Someone must get together the most influential citizens, preferably those with money that could support legal representation. The way that he directed his remark convinced Enid that she had to volunteer to try to assemble a group of potential association members. Chavez agreed to meet with them, but in the meantime to help Enid he researched the permits issued for Casa de Mastil.

He knew that the need for an environmental assessment, zoning approval and a building permit for every structure near the coast was clearly defined in both local and federal statutes. He reported to Enid that Pedro had only prepared the assessment after the fact and that he had only one almost legal building permit: the bogus copy that he showed to Enid. There was no legal master plan. One was required before any building permits could be issued for Casa de Mastil. When one of the less cooperative county officials required such from Pedro, he had gone to the state offices and, after appropriate payoffs, received a back-dated permit for a master plan of all the units built at Casa de Mastil. The officials apparently failed to notice that the Casa de Mastil described in the approval was actually located on a piece of land in the remote hamlet of Vista Mar.

Enid approached every person that attended the Chavez party. She got their nodding approval to support a Santa Rita association to preserve the environment. Unfortunately, the Mexicans that had been urged to join the action group distrusted the Gringos and the local Mexicans distrusted those from Mexico City whom they called *Chilangos* behind their backs. The local Mexicans promptly withdrew from the association to form their own group. Their departure was not so much a protest as it was a difference of interests. They wanted to solve the problems of water supply and build better schools. They could also see the disadvantage of trying to run a single meeting in two different languages.

The split meant that funds necessary to start the association were never raised. Enid was one of the prime losers in the short history of the association. The large concrete framework below her was being progressively filled with glass walls and bright yellow plastered surfaces. Each floor level was divided and sold despite the fact that construction of the next level was still underway. Every day, Enid's once uninterrupted view of the Pacific was being more obscured.

Grant England returned to the States convinced of Pedro's ruthless disregard for any law, temporal or otherwise. Grant hired an attorney he knew in San Diego. The California location was picked because Grant wanted Pedro charged for breach of contract under United States laws rather than under an unfamiliar Mexican legal system. To build his case, Grant introduced himself over the phone and said that he'd heard that Enid had some misgivings about Pedro. Would she help him in his lawsuit with any facts she had about Pedro's deals. Importantly, he needed to establish that Peter and Eugenia Sessions were conducting business in the United States, much of it in California. Enid signed a deposition that showed that her construction funds had been deposited in a Bank of America account in San Diego. She further stated that Pedro had advertised in Colorado that her villa was for sale; and that she had talked more than once with Pedro about her villa's construction when he was staying at his condominium in Palm Springs.

Grant got other owners to describe their construction problems and he asked the sport fishing boat skipper to tell about his dealings with Pedro. Grant's attorney filed a suit that described Pedro's nefarious character and his numerous financial transactions in California. Pedro's attorneys responded to the charges with a brief claiming that the bank account was merely a means to transfer dollars into his Mazatlan bank. Further, any contacts with villa owners while at his Palm Springs condo were purely social. He was only there with his family during school vacations. Moreover, the attorney claimed that his client, Mr. Sessions, was ever ready to build the 3 bedroom unit for Grant at the spot they'd agreed upon. He'd never said that that spot wouldn't be on top of a high-rise.

The San Diego judge spent little time considering the opposing testimonies. He spoke to Grant:

"I have a year's backlog of lawsuits to catch up with. Although the complainant seems to have a case, I want him to settle it in Mexico where the actual breach occurred. If you cannot get satisfaction there, you may bring the suit back here."

Once again, Pedro Sessions had escaped a legal bind. The thought that Grant might actually try to take his suit to Mexico prompted Pedro to have his Mexican attorney prepare a preemptive suit charging Grant with defamation of character and, as exampled by his lack of winning the suit in San Diego, false accusations.

Casa de Mastil's new road, that he'd earlier described as the Tunnel of Love, was causing Pedro some headaches. An occasional lost tourist, or guests from the bed and breakfast up the hill, used his road as a short cut to the beach. The owner of the Madera B & B above him was always complaining about Pedro's guests blocking her parking area or the excessive noise when the Casa de Cabra was used for a fiesta. Limiting their access to the road would be a form of retaliation for the bothersome neighbor. In truth, Pedro had a growing paranoia about security that might presumably be for the hotel guests, but was actually about imagined threats to him. He ordered his masons to construct sixteen foot high stone obelisks at either side of the entrance to Casa de Cabra. They installed steel plate hinge pin brackets to hold what was without doubt the largest pair of gates in the state of Sinaloa. The basic metalwork on the gates was a series of vertical pickets support-ing intertwined "anchor" chains. In the middle of each gate, however, was a wrought iron circle that contained a contrived Casa de Mastil logo.

The new gates didn't stop foot traffic from entering the hotel property. "Tres-passers" soon learned to walk around the massive stone pylons. Pedro first took care of this by installing three bands of barbed wire across openings on either side of the gates. This was standard practice for the new foreigners that were marking their bounds making the entire town of Santa Rita look like a collection of sheep paddocks. Local Mexicans that had for centuries walked freely around their ejido laughed as they cut away the Gringos *Guardas* to keep ancient pathways open. Pedro kept adding more wire until Casa de Cabra looked more like a Gulag than an exclusive resort.

Inside the wire, however, a network of palms, ficus, bougainvillea and hibiscus was turning Enid's villa into a near-paradise. Her La Arboleda was just one of the similarly built, and definitely intriguing, villas that in themselves could create a special place. They collectively provided a Norte Americano quality of life without destroying the Mexican ambience. All this was negated as the new tower grew taller. Some said that it was just another example of Pedro's greed for more income.

Enid began to see it as his equal greed, as a designer, to do the biggest project in Santa Rita. This was the Sessions' version of the Empire State Building. Enid knew, however, that her anger wasn't just about his high-rise. It was about breaking a trust. It was about destroying her faith that Casa de Mastil would be built out as it had begun. It was about the Peter Principal. Pedro had risen and finally reached his level of incompetence.

In contrast, 'Juan's and Rusty's development further along the beach was proceeding like a well-planned military operation. Juan used his web of business contacts to raise ample funds to build a Santa Rita resort palace. That same business provided him with a small army of disciplined and willing workers. Rusty's experience in real estate sales made the team complete. He knew that their immediate task was to win over support for their project from the entire Santa Rita community. They started with informal parties on the beach, where the more vocal citizens could voice their opinions and the developers could answer them with conciliatory changes.

"Of course we don't want a tower. The rumors are nonsense. Nothing shall be taller than the palm trees along the beach. We will save each one and add more." There was also the chance to do some subliminal market studies.

"We haven't decided upon a name. What would you call the finest resort in Sinaloa? No, the greatest resort on the Pacific Coast! The Riviera? That might be it!"

Word of the gatherings spread easily through the small Gringo community and soon Juan's parties became just as popular as the ones he held decades before. This time, however, the trip-inducing stimulants had been replaced with Margaritas and beach barbeques. Enid was pleased to be included when neighbors urged her to join them at one of what were being dubbed the Riviera Roundups. There she met the two promoters and found willing listeners to her tales of trouble at Casa de Mastil. She was also impressed by Rusty's honesty and Juan's easy manner as a host.

"Wouldn't you like to join me for a freshly caught lobster? My associates and I dove for them this afternoon and I can assure you of their quality."

Enid accepted, observing that Juan could afford to be gracious with so much excellent help. Behind an improvised serving table, she saw two men dressed in white tee shirts and black slacks. Each of them wore web belts over their tee shirts that held silvery knives. Juan saw her looking at them.

"Oh, my boys are never without them! They use those knives to pry loose oysters, open the lobsters or butcher and bone the barbeques."

20

Walkers wandering west along the Santa Rita beach could still kick up a glitter of gold from the iron pyrite in the black volcanic sands, but the granite face of the cliff at Punta Santa Rita was now obscured. In its place was a different gold, the jaundiced yellow walls of Pedro Sessions' high-rise. Townspeople muttered to each other.

"He has overloaded our sewers, he has taken our water, and he is stealing our view. What next?"

"Stealing Santa Rita!"

The new owner of level two of the high-rise was just as upset with Pedro, but for different reasons. Ed Seifert had made a deal with Pedro to buy the loft space "as is" so that Ed could personally supervise the interior finishes. Ed was a contractor and home builder. He knew that he could buy materials and equipment far cheaper from his own suppliers. He had retired but liked a chance to still be in the game. On his first auto trip south from his home in Durango, Colorado, Ed dragged a U-Drive rental trailer. It was filled with a Thermador propane gas range and barbecue, a combination GE refrigerator-freezer, two Kohler extended-front water closets and a six foot diameter Jacuzzi hot tub. Ed thought that he had made a good real estate bargain.

Pedro was not pleased when he saw Ed's refrigerator-freezer blatantly standing free against a kitchen wall. Pedro had specified unobtrusive, undercounter refrigerators for all his other units. One of Pedro's design trademarks was to obscure the sight of any mechanical or electrical device. Perhaps he had just forgotten to consider them in his original visions. It was probably more a result of his many years of living an expatriate surfer's life. During those early years in the Casa de Cabra he never had stoves, refrigerator freezers or washing machines. He became oblivious to mechanical and electrical equipment. He simply didn't know that it was needed.

Ed made his second trip south to meet a truck in Laredo that had towed his 30 foot fishing boat, PRONTO, from Florida. As one of his deals with Pedro, he proposed trading sixty percent interest in the boat for a $ 50,000 share of the purchase price of Level 2. The idea appealed to Pedro because he could forget the Yacht Club fiasco and picture himself as a real boat owner: not quite a J.P. Morgan or Commodore Vanderbilt but enough to bring him respect around Punta Viento Resort. The purchase agreement required that Pedro meet Ed at the border where the boat would be transferred to a Mexican truck and trailer. This freed Ed, as the then minor owner, from Mexican custom duties or trouble with the transfer of title records. Pedro never showed up at the border.

Ed was damned if he was going to send the boat back to Florida. He decided to take it himself into Mexico on a temporary visitor's pass and rehired the truck and trailer for the trip to the Mazatlan marina. He left the driver and rig there while he sought out Pedro. He finally found him at the resort Tennis Club and waited out six games until Pedro finally won the set with his usual drop shot.

"It just slipped my mind. We knew you were coming with the boat but I'd forgotten that I was supposed to meet you. I do have a new idea for you. Instead of all that messy paperwork, why don't you lease the boat to Eugenia? ."

"Will she maintain it, be responsible for any risks in chartering, carry the insurance and hire a full time skipper?"

"Of course. Genie loves boats!" This way, Pedro didn't have to commit himself or come up with import duty money that he never had in the first place. He had a reason for not going to the border.

Ed leased a berth at the marina, paid the first month's docking fee and spent the next two weeks supervising the finish work in his new unit. Just before he returned to Colorado, he got Pedro to agree to hire a competent seafarer named Jack Petrie to operate and maintain the boat.

Two months later Ed returned to Santa Rita and dropped off a load of decorating materials. He then drove to the marina with the intent of spending the night on his—now mostly Eugenia's—boat. At the marina he stopped to get his bearings. The boat wasn't in its slip. He found the Harbormaster to ask if Jack P. was out with the PRONTO.

"Oh, no. Jack never got paid so he quit. The slip fee was two months overdue so we had to move it to the public pier. It's over there."

Ed's eyes followed the pointed finger. At the public dock he could see that the PRONTO was sitting low in the water because no one had bothered to operate the bilge pumps as it sat there through the summer rains. He could guess that the hold was completely under water so that the batteries were probably ruined. His biggest concern was that salt water intrusion might have damaged the diesel engines. Truly worried, he told Pedro that the boat must be hauled out of the marina for repairs and made up a list of instructions.

- *I don't know how you can do it without a knowledgeable person like Jack P., but it will take three people to do the job: Someone in the boat, a driver, and number 3 to hitch up the pull cable.*

- *You must have a powerful truck to get four tons up a boat ramp. It needs good brakes and needs a connection to tie to the trailer brakes.*

- *Do not rent a trailer. Use the one I brought down or you will injure the thru-hull transponders and damage the Furuno 1650 and the Low Range 150. They cost $1,000 to replace.*

- *Hire a local diver to scrape the hull before the haul-out. If the growth dries out, you could ruin the fiberglass surface by trying to scrape it off.*

- *Make sure the engines are treated for out of water storage. Jack P. was going to do it so you must hire an experienced person or come up with $25,000 to replace them.*

- *he storage yard must have good security to protect the auto pilot, GPS, depth recorders and fish finder.*

When Ed went to see how his instructions had been followed, he found the boat with a dirty hull, standing in an open lot behind Pedro's place in Punta Viento. The batteries were dead, the engines rusting. It hardly fit on a strange, flimsy trailer. Pedro had sold Ed's to pay for the haul-out.

It was not hard for Gringos to meet in Santa Rita. Two walkers passing on the dusty roads could hardly avoid greetings. Friendships formed easily for foreign homeowners whose minority status encouraged a bond. Thus, Enid met Ed and the two were soon comparing their Pedro problems. Enid talked about her inability to sell and Ed described his problems with the boat. Each of them was worried about the high-rise.

Enid told Ed that she had no chance to sell until Regularization took place, and she thought that Pedro was purposely holding up the process until the high-rise was completed. She had heard a rumor that, once this was done, all of the properties would be melded into one condominium association. This would be Pedro's answer to the rising concerns by owners about title to their units. Moreover it would put all the outside land and utilities into common ownership so that Pedro could forget about them. Enid would then become partly responsible to correct all the mistakes that Pedro had made with the hotel.

Ed had a more complex problem. Whereas Enid's villa sat alone, Ed's unit was the second level of the multi-story tower. Apportioning the cost of shared utilities and solving common operating problems was going to be difficult in a building where those things were never considered in the design. Ed also was worrying about what was being built above his level. How high was Pedro going to go? Was the structure safe?

Animosity against Pedro had spread amongst the villa owners as they got to know each other and shared their common concerns. One was about water. Some couldn't believe that a shortage was already there when Pedro built his units. Others had heard that sea water was beginning to infiltrate the aquifer that supplied the town well. It was hard, still, to believe there was a problem when Pedro seemed to be solving it. Near the new road he installed a massive concrete cistern and faced the box with a brick wall that stepped with each course from a pool below to the top of the box. Water continually flowed from jets at the top over the brick "waterfall" to be captured in the pool and then recirculated. The construction not only shouted abundance but also provided a pleasing sound of splash to passersby. Few knew that Pedro had used up his year's water quota and that the cistern was filled during the night by a tank truck bringing water from Mazatlan.

Water posed a different threat for Enid. Because she was near the top of the hill she often had dry faucets when other users drained the supply tank. The system worked well when she first occupied La Arboleda, but it suffered when more villas were constructed below her. Like the frequent power shortages, dry faucets seemed just the price you had to pay for living in near-Paradise.

Pedro solved her water shortages without burdening her with the details. In October, Enid returned to find a new, three-foot square concrete box installed near her guest room. Her usual peace was now shattered with the sound of a pump located in the box. Enid called down to the office to complain about the noise. Eventually it stopped. At the time, she was happy to have a daughter and her son-in-law in Santa Rita for a week of swimming and surfing. The three of them were seated near the pool when they heard a sound from the guest bedroom. A sheet of water was gushing out from the room completely filling the meter-wide opening.

Enid called down to the desk again, excitedly describing a bad flood from the guest room.

"It's an emergency. Please send help immediately."

The pump in the box began to hum again and the deluge stopped. One of the house cleaners arrived after two hours, too late to clean up the deluge.

Enid's son-in-law was worried about how all this had happened. He discovered a new PVC pipe that led from the space below the deck to the box and a similar pipe leaving the box. He looked in the guest room under the bed and found a square concrete access panel that was still leaking water around its edges. When they put it all together, Enid remembered seeing the panel during construction. Pedro had told her that it was to be a water storage tank but that he'd abandoned the idea when she bought all the building. Now he realized that he had a plumbing problem. His existing system pumped water from his waterfall to a cistern above the Casa de Cabra. The existing pump couldn't keep up with the demand from all his new units, so Pedro had opened Enid's tank again as a staging reservoir from which he could pump to the cistern on top of the hill. That involved two pumps. When Enid complained about the noise, the concierge had shut off the pump in the box, but no one had shut down the pump that supplied Enid's tank from the waterfall.

The next day a quieter pump was installed. Enid would have forgotten the matter if Pedro hadn't secretly hooked up the pump to her power panel. One night her power supply was shut down but not that to the rest of the hotel and the water-fall. When her power failed, the local pump shut down while the pump from the waterfall continued to operate. She woke to again hear the gushing sound and called down to the front desk. There was no answer. The flood continued until daybreak.

Enid envisioned renters with young children in the guest room. What would happen if they awoke scared in the night by the flood, rushed out the door and slipped on the smooth concrete near the pool? Drowning? Of course it was possible. That morning Enid pulled the hotel manager out of a staff meeting and threatened to personally remove the pump and pipes.

"The danger is obvious. We could all be sued. Why did you use that tank without my permission?"

"It was always there," the manager answered.

In another incident, the front desk called Enid to say that the lower road gates had to be shut and she should use the upper gates until further notice. That night she dutifully went out the top gate but on her return found it secured with a pad-lock. She had to drive the rutted roads the long way back into town and then along the beach in order to hopefully find a security guard. When she did, he helplessly held out his hands to say that even the lower gate had been locked at its very top and he had no ladder to open it. Enid walked up the 152 steps to her villa and sat down at the computer stand near her bed to write a letter of com-plaint. In the midst of the first sentence, she was stopped by a threatening noise. The heavy iron chandelier over her bed had pulled loose from its rusted mount-ing and dropped right where she usually slept.

The gate closing was prompted by Ed's parking habits. He was both the fault and the victim. His agreement with Pedro guaranteed him a parking place and origi-nally he had pulled up close to the entrance to his unit in order to lessen the strain on his arthritic legs. Suddenly the gates were shut and the parking space guaranteed to Ed was planted with more grass.

"Automobiles detract from the beauty of my Kissing Lawn!" was Pedro's explana-tion for the closure.

Seifert was learning that his supposed bargain with Pedro was beginning to back-fire, or more correctly was being repaid in kind. Ed's agreement gave him the rights to the entire level 2. Accordingly, he constructed two storage units and a laundry room in his hallway, only to find that the hotel had usurped one of his storage rooms. Pedro said,

"You don't need that much storage."

Enid and Ed were amongst those attending one of Juan's beach parties. Despite the good food and drinks and the need to listen briefly to Juan or Rusty describe their progress on the Riviera Resort, their conversation soon returned to Pedro Sessions. At one point they made a vow to accept a fine if either ever again mentioned his name. The fine penalty didn't last long because at each meeting there were more examples to discuss.

21

Enid came to Santa Rita to escape the gray days in Steamboat that fell between the Harvest moon and Thanksgiving. These were the days after the green had disappeared and before the entire countryside came up white. Ed Seibert arrived soon after from Durango. The two had formed a friendship, albeit one welded together by a common dislike of Peter Oliver Sessions. As a break away from their usual discussion topic, Enid had suggested that the two go into town for dinner at Ramón's. Their travel was interrupted by a crowd watching a parade to celebrate the Feast of the Miracle of Guadalupe.

They chatted with other Gringos on the street and learned that the Miracle occurred on a barren hill called Tepeyac in the year 1531. There a recent convert to Catholicism named Juan Diego swore to a priest that he had seen the Virgin Mary. The priest asked for some kind of proof.

Juan Diego just happened to see a re-appearance of the Virgin a few days later. The Virgin instructed him to pick roses from a dry and desolate hill. Juan Diego went there and found roses growing as if the place was a mission garden. He carried a bundle of the flowers to show the priest and as they fell away from his arms a perfect image of the Virgin appeared on his garment.

Tepeyac was also the site of an Aztec temple dedicated to Tonatzin, mother of their gods. The Catholic priest had recently ordered the temple demolished. His recent converts saw the Miracle as both sanctifying their former temple and proving the existence of the new god described by the priest. All of this added up to making the Virgen de Guadalupe the Queen of Mexico and good reason for a parade and fireworks to follow.

Enid and Ed stood beside the Independencia and watched as the more affluent fishermen, farmers and real estate brokers became *Charros*. A dozen of them rode their horses in formation up the street and then kept them in a positioned gait. The mounted escort was waiting for a flower-smothered float to catch up. When it did, Enid picked out the symbolic figures. What might have otherwise been the homecoming queen stood wrapped in layers of a gauze-like fabric bravely trying to stay erect as the float truck bumped its way up the cobbled road. She was obviously depicting the Virgin and the young man beside her was dressed as the priest. Sitting unhappily at the front of the float was a boy, dressed as Juan Diego, that couldn't wait until he could get the ice cream promised him at the end of the event.

Enid and Ed proceeded to Ramón's, a new restaurant that was jointly owned by the Mexican chef and the son of a San Diego banker. It occupied a corner where the major road from the plaza met the beach. The ground floor held a long bar and a few dining tables for those that walked in from the beach. Enid and Ed climbed a short flight of stairs and found themselves under a huge roof that looked as if had been put together by watchmakers. All of the log supports were straight and smooth and held together with rawhide ropes. The log spacing was regular and the palm frond in-fill looked as if it had been woven on a loom. This was no Pedro palapa. They picked a table with a view of the beach and ocean and checked the menu. Enid asked for *Camerones Sautéed* in garlic and butter. Ed ordered the fish of the day, Dorado, and was happy to see that Ramón hadn't tried to trick tourists by calling it Mahi-Mahi. The Hawaiian name seemed to be appearing on every other menu along the coast. As each drank a Pacifico beer, they easily forgot their vow not to discuss topic *Pedro*. Enid was the first to speak.

"The villagers are really upset. He put that fancy paving all across the front of the hotel and it looks like he's trying to acquire the public road through intimidation. This is their access to the cemetery and the beach, but they are scared to use it. To add to their worry, he planted new grass areas on the beach side of the road and filled them with green umbrellas, white cast iron tables and chairs. Add the patterned paving and it looks like the hotel owns everything. It makes the villagers feel like they are trespassing on private property when it's really theirs!"

"It's all part of his way of taking without paying. He entices Gringos to his restaurant because it's pleasant to be served under the trees and listen to the sea lick at his new stone wall. Of course he doesn't own any of it!"

"The restaurant? He now has found someone to lease the space. I've eaten there and the food is good."

"But the chef told me that people won't come back because there's no place to park. How is Pedro going to sell more units without parking?"

Their more serious conversation was about the ever-growing high-rise. Originally, the ground level served as a parking garage. During the summer Pedro had turned this level into three rental units with glass, ocean-view doors surrounded by an elaborate façade of curved moldings and Corinthian-capped pilasters. The new grass area and paved road made first-time guests think they had a room with a private, paved deck connecting them directly to the waterfront. The first truck that went by filled with laughing children quickly changed their minds.

Pedro had pre-sold levels 3 and 4 above Ed and Manuel his men working on final finishes. The ceiling slab of level 5 was in place and they were now building forms for levels 6 and 7. Enid had watched Pedro lead prospects onto the bare slabs and describe with waving arms where their units would be. She knew that Ed thought he'd outwitted the man and gone into the purchase with his eyes open; but he now confessed that he'd made a mistake. They both had the problem with clear titles, but this multi-story building put Ed's ownership even more in question. If you didn't own everything down to the ground, what did you own? The rumors about making the hotel into a condominium were just that.

The next day Ed became curious about progress on all the floors above him. He couldn't check from the outside because Pedro had draped green netting over all the unfinished floors. The front desk explained that the netting was there to hide what was a typical construction mess from the guests. Ed was surprised to see that there was no activity. Forms were only half-finished and the exposed reinforcing bars had begun to rust. The truth was that construction had stopped. Manuel realized that the multi-story construction was getting him in over is head, and he had insisted that Pedro hire an engineer for technical advice. The engineer was shocked to find out that Pedro was adding levels with a structural scheme that was meant for one and two story buildings. The engineer brought in a building inspector that ordered Pedro to halt construction. The green netting was there to hide illegal interior work on the floors that had been pre-sold.

For the next few months, Enid waited for the eyesore to be improved and Ed waited out life in an unfinished building. Pedro had other concerns. Some villa owners were sure that he had permanently moved to Punta Viento to avoid contact with Santa Rita's outraged citizens. Most were happy to see him go. Perhaps he had taken their advice to get out of hotel operations and concentrate on using his design skills. Pedro had followed that advice to a point. He hired a new hotel manager who was allowed to siphon off complaints but had to report directly to him for all decisions. He didn't want the kind of independent thinking that he'd had with Jeff Woods. Woods by this time was no longer at Casa de Mastil. He had seen the folly in trying to operate a hotel when he was continually second-guessed by Pedro. He returned to coaching tennis. The new manager, Imelda Buchanan, was an expatriate from Chile. Lithe without being skinny, Imelda always received a second look from men. Close up, they found that the manager had a steely attraction that held the attention of guests and commanded respect from other employees. Imelda had left Chile to be trained in hotel management at the University of Denver. She then headed south to Mexico where her fluent Spanish and gracious manner was quickly put to work in the Hotel Playa Mazatlan. Pedro had first met her there while he was attending a conference of Evangelical laymen. The subject of the conference was, *Finding Christ in the Business World.*

Imelda brought new hope to the villa owners that she would keep them informed about events at the hotel. Pedro had never done this. It covered up his lack of training for a service industry and confirmed his determination not to commit anything to writing. Imelda did give out some information. She described why the repairs were necessary that were charged for on an owner's quarterly statement. She gave the first status report on the process of Regularization and the Condominium Regime. In one message, she proudly announced that the hotel would now accept credit cards. Because Pedro had always wanted to avoid the 4 or 5% charge from the card companies he had never accepted anything except Pesos as payment by guests. Because the hotel had no established credit record, Imelda's plan to allow Visa, Master Card and American Express transactions never transpired.

She learned quickly that her responsibilities were limited to day-to-day operations but that she was the one that had to explain why when Pedro raised management fees or curtailed some services. This brought her the nickname of The Dragon Lady, the beautiful but ruthless woman featured in the now defunct *Terry and the Pirates* comic strip.

Pedro moved his *jefe*, Manuel, to new work in Punta Viento, and promoted Paulo to replace Manuel as foreman on the high-rise. It wasn't long before Pedro ordered Imelda to summarily fire the English-speaking plumber with the excuse that Paulo was using the high-rise crew to build a house for Paulo's in-laws. It didn't matter that it was on a Sunday and that Paulo was paying the men directly. What was really behind the firing was the fact that Paulo, by law, was accruing a large bonus that was guaranteed him by the government. Pedro didn't want to pay it so he invented a cause for dismissal and eliminated his obligation for bonuses, overtime or severance pay.

The move to Punta Viento was close to permanent when compared to all of Pedro's previous relocations. While the signs faded on the closed Santa Rita real estate office and dust settled over the desk, Pedro was opening a new office at the end of the Punta Viento beach. There were no identifying signs outside the space and few real estate sales items inside, as if Pedro was somehow engaged in illicit trade. Although some may have explained the sparse office as a sign of Pedro's reserve, few understood that it was all part of the Sessions' business plan. Pedro never "sold" real estate. He sold himself. Everyone that bought anything from him seemed to do it almost as an afterthought, a token of gratitude for all the attention paid during a whirlwind promotional visit. The obscure office was a perfect place to disguise the sting when you dropped in to say goodbye. Of course, after the check was signed, he dropped any form of friendliness.

Enid and Ed often wondered as they talked whether an experienced psychiatrist could analyze such an ironic character. Was Pedro just the victim of numerous personality conflicts, a hardened schemer, just plain dumb..... or all of these. His flirts with the law, even the sometimes lax Mexican law, were increasing. Did he look at life as just a series of surfing waves: some great rides, some duds that threw you around? The bad ones passed and there was always a great one coming. Ed pondered this and then asked,

"Why did he create a property with the unique ambience of Casa de Mastil and then make it just another real estate deal? Was it simply money greed to permit him to live with the super-rich in Punta Viento or the drive of a frustrated artist to build a bigger monument. Where does Eugenia fit in all of this? Is she just a victim of a bad marriage, but hanging on to protect her son? On the other hand, is she the power behind the greed, pushing Pedro to satisfy her hunger for a richer life? How did this Aphrodite end up out of historical sync with a Napoleon?" Enid added her questions.

"Did you hear that he was being sued again? There's talk that he's making millions and sending it offshore and that he'll skip to Belize or Guatemala. All I know is that he's selling off everything he can in Santa Rita; but still wants to hang on to his income from the rental commissions."

"Although he has a few unsold units, Pedro is in complete charge of the hotel's finances," Ed added. "He can manipulate expenses, short-change services and avoid the costs of upkeep even though he doesn't own any of the properties. One day I tried to estimate how much he's diverting from the hotel income. The occupancy rate for the last two years was around 46% or a total of 170 days. This would bring in commissions averaging $300,000. Management fees totaled $140,000. A conservative estimate of expenses was put at under $240,000. He could be taking as much as $200,000 from the hotel without any effort on his part."

When Enid returned in January she found that nothing had happened with the high-rise except that a coat of red lead had been painted over the rusting reinforcing rods. They stuck up above every column supporting level 7. The skeletal red rods and the green screening created a giant artifact that sort of celebrated Christmas when it should be observing the Day of the Dead. She didn't know that, no matter what his end goal was for the tower, Pedro was just following a Mexican tradition: property taxes would not be levied until a project was completed.

She met Ed in front of the high-rise and he suggested a walk on the beach. He wanted to talk to her about his current troubles with Casa de Mastil. Apparently, Ed's constant bickering about operating expenses and lack of parking spaces was beginning to weaken Imelda's service smile. She listened to him complain that she had rented his unit to hotel guests for half the normal rate.

"We had to move them out of a flooded villa and give them a special rate. Your unit was open," Imelda explained. "Would you rather forfeit the income?" Ed accepted her explanation but lost his argument that Pedro didn't deserve his 35% commission.

Ed said that he was worried about getting a legal title but, when he arrived, there was no news from Pedro. Then he heard that his nemesis had hired a detailed survey of all the units in the hotel. The surveyor told Pedro that his tower was in fact slightly intruding on neighboring property. Pedro replied that his former surveyor had made an honest mistake. His lawyer would take care of the minor problem. Ed wondered if Pedro was beginning to see a possible advantage to a Condominium Regime. If all the property was transferred into the names of all the other complainers, they as the owners would be the ones liable for injuries or any other problems from construction defects or legal entanglements.

When Ed learned about the survey and its possible use to establish the condo regime he asked Imelda for a look at the engineer's description for his unit. When she refused, he got the front desk to make him a copy. He found that the survey didn't include the storage closets and laundry room that were, by agreement, his property. Hoping to compare notes, with other owners Ed offered the concierge a tip for a list of their names. He told Enid that his reward was a copy of an E-mail from Imelda to Pedro stating,

"He must be stopped. He was seen urinating off his balcony by the night watchman. He stole a document from the office that was seen in his unit by a maid. He tried to bribe the concierge. He is parking illegally on our Kissing lawn. We have called the police."

Imelda convinced the police to tow the car. When Ed saw his SUV being taken away, he rushed out of his unit to discuss the matter with the police. Two men in dark uniforms were sitting in their white pickup truck while a third stood in the back with his riot gun slung over a shoulder. They had no idea why the vehicle was illegally parked, but said that their duty was simply to follow it to the tow lot. They said that, once there, if Ed paid the towing charge he could get back his SUV.

"That is the procedure, *SENOR*," they assured him," and there is no way it can be cut short."

22

Despite what seemed to be a healthy income from the hotel, Pedro needed more financing for his new project near the Punta Viento Resort. He found it with two brothers, Jerry and Bob Misrack. Each had put down deposits of $60,000 that guaranteed them each half of Level 6 in the tower. They'd heard nothing about the high-rise problems and didn't worry that their floor was still unfinished, but they were sure they were going to have the best views in Santa Rita. They were so impressed with Pedro's designs for the hotel that they agreed to put an equal amount into the Punta Viento project. This allowed Manuel to continue with the construction of a large, luxury villa facing the ocean.

Pedro's design for the villa echoed his early creative work at Casa de Mastil. Many of the walls were curved to form sleeping and dining spaces and he installed Jacuzzi tubs as well as showers in each bathroom. Marble replaced the concrete he'd used for counter tops in Santa Rita and large glass doors in hard-wood frames opened to the bay views. A swimming pool stood on the edge of a large paved terrace and a wine cellar was built where the land sloped away under the terrace. When finished, the villa was offered for sale but was also made available to rent for $10,000 US per week. There were no buyers and few renters.

Pedro convinced his partners that the villa needed to look lived in and that Genie and their son had agreed to help with this marketing ploy. Genie filled her role as a smiling, devoted wife thrilled to live in her husband's creation. That was as far as she got. She was kept out of any further involvement as Pedro selected every piece of furniture and artifact in every room of the villa. He dictated where coffee table ornaments were placed and what flowers could be put in vases that he'd chosen and carefully located on teak cabinets. At first Genie accepted this as his designer's privilege as interior decorator. Then she realized every move was deliberate. Pedro was developing a compulsion for order. Whenever he was at home he spent his time in the villa straightening every picture, making bathroom towels all hang at the same height and moving back a decorative bowl or plate that Genie might have misplaced to the exact spot he'd originally chosen for it. This new trait bothered Genie. She knew that it was more than another manifestation of Pedro's artistic drive.

Ed wasn't happy that his boat had been dragged to the new villa. As a supposed thirty per cent owner, he had a right to use the boat and to expect that it would be properly maintained. Pedro assumed that he was released from worries by insisting that the boat be leased to Genie. He had no interest in using the craft and had neglected to have it registered in Mexico. Pedro considered it Ed's problem. As he had failed to follow any of the detailed maintenance instructions, Ed asked for help from the Harbor Master and a local police officer. The three of them arrived at the entrance to Pedro's gated community. A guard at the gate refused them entry without Pedro's permission. He called the villa for Pedro's authorization to admit the task force. A voice stated that he was not in residence. As the police officer discussed the legalities, the enclave gates opened wide and a Cherokee SUV rushed through them and disappeared down the road to Santa Cruz. Hunched behind the wheel was Peter Oliver Sessions.

As Norte Americanos returned for the winter season, they were shocked to see the extent of what many were calling Pedro's Folly. The tower loomed out at the end of the beach with its new yellow paint job obscuring the sight of what was once a familiar cliff. The permanent Gringo residents, the seasonal arrivals and even the old family Mexicans were beginning to unite in their distaste for a project that they were sure didn't conform to the local planning and zoning codes. They also worried that, if Pedro's tower was allowed by the government, Juan and Rusty or anyone else would have legal license to do the same thing.

Slowly, some of the residents began to discuss ways to revive the aborted citizen's group. They asked Enid if she would try again to form an association. At first she was reluctant to get involved, believing that some might question her dedication to the community because her villa was for sale. Then she realized that her chances for selling the villa would be better if the high-rise was stopped and rallying the community against massive construction might be a step in the right direction. With Nancy's help she approached most of the original group and urged them to reconsider supporting a plan of action. Her purposely general plan suggested these areas of concern:

1. Zoning (control Santa Rita's growth)

2. Water (improve quality and supply)

3.   Beach Access (preserve historic rights of way)

4.   Sewer (extend sewer pipes to all of Santa Rita)

At first reading her proposal received little support from the group. The problems of organization hadn't changed. The native Mexicans still distrusted those Mexicans that had moved to Santa Rita from Mexico City. The Gringos were divided between the NAPS (North American Pioneers) that wanted to keep the village as a hamlet and the NIPS (Newly-Invested People) that were only interested in building bigger and bigger second homes. Enid knew she needed to pull them together and said,

"To do this we need someone like Dr. Chavez. He has told me that if the money can be raised, he will prepare the necessary papers to make a new, legal association. The new association will be a bona fide voice for Santa Rita and it will have the right to force the government to act in favor of the community."

"But, how can it exist without the support of the village?" one of the Mexican's responded. "They have seen that the old association was ineffective and have little faith that anyone in the government will listen or act without greasing palms."

"If we could start with just one action that would show our power, the village will see that the association has strength." Enid suddenly had an idea. "To show the community that the association has power, it could first attack the worst eyesore in town."

"You mean the high-rise?" someone asked.

"Well, yes, many of us that look at it would be willing to pay to see construction stopped and perhaps even see some floors taken down. I think I could raise enough funds to start the association if the first action will be against Pedro Sessions."

"With all due respect, we're not interested in helping those people that were stupid enough to buy into Casa de Mastil," muttered one of the NAPS "The town needs better streets, better sewers, better water supply and Casa de Mastil can go to Hell."

"You can get on your high horse," Enid replied, "but this is a quid-pro-quo. Santa Rita gets an association and we get a lower building." Others backed her up.

"I agree."

"Everyone in town is worried about being dwarfed out by these new buildings, but they don't know how to stop it."

"Everyone hates Pedro and hates his tower. This is the best way to start. I say, let her go with it."

Enid could see some of the more influential people coming around.

"To do this, we need an official organization. We need a legal set of by-laws. We need a name."

Many in the group had donated funds that were never spent for the defunct association and they suggested that those funds be transferred to the new effort. They would be used to pay Chavez for papers of incorporation. Further, he should be asked to research and report on the planning and zoning laws. Surely, they restrict building heights to three stories. A new name was agreed to. The first citizen's action group in Santa Rita would be called Citizens All United to Save the Environment: CAUSE.

Enid sent E-mail messages to Casa de Mastil owners asking each of them to contribute $1,000 to CAUSE. She noted that their views would be improved by tearing back the tower to a legal height. All of them responded, except for a new investor still charmed by Pedro's attention that thought the association was making him a whipping boy.

In April, over sixty people walked through the doors of the Ejito community center and found places in black, folding chairs set up in the main assembly room. For many it was the first time that they'd been in the building on Independencia, or even noticed the large painted sign on its white plaster street walls that proclaimed SEDE DE EJITO COMUNIDAD. Some looked up at the ceiling of the room that was made up of small brick arches supported on exposed steel beams. Others waved at friends and a few talked with their neighbors about the irony of holding a meeting in an official Mexican place without a single Mexican in attendance. By now, of course, the Mexicans had set up their own association.

The chatter stopped as Enid walked to the front of the hall accompanied by a stocky gentleman in a white shirt and dark blue trousers. He stroked his mustache as if in contemplation when Enid welcomed the group.

"I am personally pleased to see so many of you here at this first meeting of CAUSE. It is through the generous donations of some that we've been able to file legal papers for our incorporation. They have been accepted by the government in Mexico and we are now an official association. Before introducing our guest, we must cover a small detail and elect officers of the association." Nancy Devereux stood up to propose a slate with Enid as president. Her motion was seconded. The group was happy to elect anyone that would assume the burden of leading against such hopeful odds.

"Thank you for your support. The people that you have elected have worked hard over the last few months to assemble data and produce the charter for CAUSE. We could not have done it without the help of my new, good friend Doctor Ernesto Chavez. Without further talk, I would like to introduce him to you now." Those that had met Dr.Chavez before applauded as he stood before them.

"Thank you for your kindness. I am happy to return to beautiful Santa Rita, this time as a consultant to an official body that will have standing to be heard in Mexico. It is important to have a legal entity if there is any action to be taken." He stroked back black hair that had fallen over his brow. He said that at Enid's suggestion he had prepared a report on conditions as they presently existed for the community of Santa Rita. His assistant, sitting in the middle of the front row, turned on a computer and projected the first image of a Power Point presentation. As he talked, he showed official tables and maps that he said had been prepared by the federal government and were the laws at that moment in place. Other data spoke for itself. The highlights that flashed on the screen were:

Population: The approved Urban Development Plan allows a possible increase to just under **60,000** compared with the approximately **3000** full and part-time residences currently in Santa Rita.

Hotels: The Zoning Plan allows a possible **8000** rooms to be built in a **6 Story Wall** lining the beachfront.

Water Supply: The town well does not even have a capacity to serve present residents. The present Ejito water authority is threatened by outside agencies eager to confiscate Santa Rita's natural watershed to serve expansion in other parts of Sinaloa.

Waste Removal: The sewage plant is obsolete. Human waste pipes are overflowing and polluting the sea water within 200 yards of Casa de Mastil. There are no toilet facilities for the thousands that descend on the village for surfing events or during Semana Santa.

Public Access: Access to beaches is assured by Mexican law. It is being denied by arbitrary street closures. The intimation of forbidden entry comes from those stretches of sand where the Federal government has given permits to build food palapas and umbrella stands and the private paving of public ways.

Building Regulations: The laws contain very specific controls on heights, set-backs from neighbors and streets and densities for different zones.

"I understand that there is a possible plan to attack the sewer problem," Chavez quickly said as he finished his report. Ed was in the audience and was the first to get up and ask,

"Does this mean that Pedro's tower is legal if he keeps it at six stories?"

"Yes and no," Chavez replied. "The tower is in the CUC zone that allows six stories, but part of it intrudes into the Zona Federale where any construction is strictly forbidden." Chavez was quick to explain that he was investigating all aspects of the tower, but had nothing to say publicly about it.

"You say we could have Casa de Mastil towers built all along the beachfront," someone responded. "How could that happen?"

"The Federal government owes the state of Sinaloa the same opportunities for tourism that it has given Cancun. The state needs the money. All of the regulations were prepared with this in mind by architects and planners in Mexico City. They never set foot in Santa Rita."

"What can we do?" asked a newcomer that seemed to capture the sentiment of the group. There wasn't as much anger as there was disbelief that this little town could be overrun by giant hotel corporations and greedy developers. How could someone like Pedro Sessions build so many units if there was not enough water and the sewer system was defunct? Chavez spoke again to the gathering.

"Only organized social or citizen action may hope to control development by demanding first that the government enforce the details of the regulations in place and secondly that the laws in place be changed to what the community wants. This is the reason for CAUSE and I urge its support." Enid stood again before the group.

"As Dr. Chavez has so nicely pointed out, our growth problems are much greater than any of us could have even imagined. He is the only person that we know of capable of representing us in Mexico. I am now asking this group to invest Dr. Chavez with our power-of-attorney for protecting our interests on governmental matters pertaining to growth and development." There was a momentary silence as people wondered how all of a sudden they were empowered to vote on any matter, particularly on such short notice. Enid knew from the beginning that if the association was going to be born at all, she had to short cut the democratic procedures that might be expected in the States. She sensed the possible reaction brewing and took a chance, knowing it was a critical point in the life or death of the association.

"According to our by-laws this is an official meeting and the majority vote here shall determine the actions of the association. Do I hear ayes?" There were enough affirmative answers to assure her of support for the association and its first task of stopping Pedro's high-rise. With that the meeting ended.

What Chavez did not reveal at the meeting was that he was making a full investigation into the permits issued for all of Pedro's developments. He had gone to each local, county and state office that was responsible for issuing permits since the start of Casa de Mastil and made copies of every transaction. The copy file was two inches thick, but nowhere did it show any permits being issued to Peter or Isabella Eugenia Sessions except for a bogus zoning permit issued to build a project called Casa de Mastil.......in the remote village of Vista Mar!

Dr. Chavez called Enid and said, "These are not the kind of Gringos we want here. I have prepared a Popular Complaint, a lawsuit by the people."

His complaint questioned the acts of public officials that failed to enforce their own edicts and asked for fines up to $250,000 and possible jail sentences from 3 months to 12 years for Sessions. Of particular importance to Casa de Mastil owners was the request for immediate DEMOLITION of the top three floors of the tower.

Somehow Pedro must have been tipped off that Dr. Chavez was investigating Casa de Mastil. Just before the lawsuit was filed, Manuel arrived at the tower site with a dozen workers that began, like ants, to eat away the top two floors. The sledge hammers they started with made slow progress and were soon replaced with electric jack hammers. The hammers cut away a section of the concrete columns to expose the steel reinforcing. Then the columns were pulled down with ropes and their reinforcing cut about three feet off the floor level.

All the scaffolding was salvaged, painted with preservatives and stored on level 5. The workmen bent down each of the reinforcing rods that had been left exposed after the columns were removed. They could be bent up again and reused to rebuild the columns. It was apparent that Pedro intended to act as if he was complying with the law but was in fact just waiting to begin construction. There might be helpful results in the upcoming election with new officials that would support him or at least be swayed by sufficient bribes. This only made sense to Pedro because he needed level 6. He'd already taken $60,000 deposits from three different parties and promised each of them half of the floor. He did not intend to return the deposits that he'd already spent. After all, he wasn't the one that wanted the demolition. He had taken the money in good faith that level 6 would be built and he'd added level 7 after he'd double-sold level 6. It was out of his hands.

23

While CAUSE concentrated its first efforts against the high-rise at Casa de Mastil, there were larger sores festering in Santa Rita. These threats to its quiet lifestyle made even more reason that the fledgling association had to survive its initial campaign. Travel agents and tour bus operators were advertising the small town of 3000 people as an undiscovered alternative to Mazatlan's 340,000 population: what Mazatlan used to be. The ads pictured a sleepy fishing village where discriminating tourists could experience the unspoiled charm of old Mexico. The hype soon destroyed the hypothesis. Although the streets were still dusty and dogs sleeping in the roads still stalled traffic, the tourist influx now supported 31 restaurants. Granted, some were just barbeque stands on a front porch, but the town also boasted two new video rental stores and three real estate offices.

On the corner of Independencia and Dorado a sign on a tree proclaimed the area as the sanctuary of a bright green Iguana. Actually, the tree was filled with more than a dozen of the lizard-like animals. Although the *Night of the Iguana* made Puerto Vallarta famous because of its reptile population, no one paid any attention to the occupants of Santa Rita's tree. They were too busy going in and out of the boutique shops along Independencia that featured Mexico-like handicrafts imported from Indonesia.

Enid Williams made her yearly move from Steamboat Springs to Santa Rita. There she found a copy of the association's new newsletter, CAUSE, with a paragraph heading: *¿La Buena Noticias?* The good news was that the local members of the association that Enid founded were working hard in her absence. They posted fliers announcing weekly meetings at the Ejito Community Center and were slowly gaining in membership. Despite the knowledge that they were starting a campaign against the Casa de Mastil high-rise, however; there were still some bad rumors moving through the village.

"That lawyer makes too much." To a local making around $15.00 a day, $150.00 an hour sounded ridiculous.

"He's only working for the Gringos. How about finding out what the Mexicans want?" This was repeated by every person attending his or her first meeting. Unfortunately, they had never read the mission statement to understand that this was an activist organization, not a town meeting to take the political pulse of the community.

"The Association is going to make every small home owner in the central village get an environmental report before doing anything." As one of the Mexicans described the problem:

"Information is like a stone. It has many faces and it is hard to bite."

Enid faced a new problem at La Arboleda. There were an increasing number of weddings at the hotel. Most brides-to-be wanted to be married on the Kissing Lawn that had been carefully raked the morning of the wedding. If weather threatened, a large tent was erected to protect participants. On clear days four poles were dug into the grass and a gauze roof hung between the poles. A freshly picked pineapple graced the top of each pole. Here the minister, priest or rabbi stood to bind the new couple.

After the ceremony on the Kissing Lawn, Enid watched a Mariachi brass band lead the wedding party up the steep roadway to the large, paved terrace above Enid. Older guests that might have faltered on the rough rock paving were taken up last by automobile. Giant palms and temporary Kon-Tiki torches bordered the driveway that led to the terrace. Once there, the group sat down to a catered dinner with toasts and sometimes ribald comments about the new couple.

The dinner was usually consumed listening to soft melodies from the Mariachi band. Around nine o'clock, however, the band was replaced by a disc jockey that played the latest hit CD's at a multi-decibel level. The volume was so high that the constant low cycled drum beats gave her a headache. After getting her first blasting, Enid sent Imelda what she felt was a justifiable E-mail request that the volume be lowered and the music stopped before midnight. Her answer was,

"It certainly would be nicer to receive constructive feedback from you than complaints and warnings." There seemed to be a misconception about who were the owners and who were the employees.

Every morning Enid planned an early walk before the sun heated the roads. She enjoyed the quiet of the jungle that boasted giant palms and lower species whose rustling fan leaves were home to creeping vines with purple and white orchid blossoms. Often hidden to the joggers and cyclists that passed by, the red Mexican Creeper and yellow Shower of Gold added to her joys of discovery. After such a find she would return to search out the identifying pictures in a book of tropical plants and try to faithfully remember Latin names like *Antigonan leptopus* and *Galphimia glauca.*

Her usual destination was one of the smaller beaches where she could walk its length eyeing the morning's crop of cones and limpet shells without ever seeing another human. Her greatest thrill was on the morning when she watched a dozen small sea turtles move from their sandy birthplace into the surf. Those that were not devoured by larger creatures might become giant tortugas, but she knew that the turtle population was near extinction so to see any was heartening. After a swim she returned to La Arboleda.

It was *Semana Santa*, the week between palm Sunday and Easter that for some Mexicans meant seven days of religious observance but for most a Semana-long, national holiday. For the Mexican vacationers this was a week of happiness. For foreign residents it was a week of horror. Tour busses took over the limited parking spaces in town. The stores were quickly emptied of Kettle chips, Coca-Cola and the usually abundant local fruits. Students on their Spring Break added to the groups of pedestrians that took over the streets and filled every bench in the Plaza.

Beachfront restaurants sought to capture the visitor's dollar by filling the beach with carefully spaced umbrellas and white, plastic lounge chairs. The spread out furniture that suggested private ownership of the public beach forced more people into the narrow strip between umbrellas and the water's edge. Few restaurant owners benefited from the typically low-income visitors. They brought their own tortillas, frijoles, rice, chicken and large cardboard flats of beer cans.

The word had been spread among the young people: Santa Rita was more fun than Fort Lauderdale and no one carded you when you ordered a beer. Most of the locals worried that the Semana Santa invasion might be worse than that for the World's Surfing Contest held the year before. Then, ten thousand people were forced to find relief in the four portable toilets stingily supplied by the show promoters. Few stood for the wait in the long lines in front of the upright boxes. No one was arrested for defecating in any spot that was conveniently shielded from most passersby.

As Enid approached Playa los Muertos she could see that the narrow entry to the beach was blocked by pick-up trucks, SUV's and dusty sedans with license plates from far away points like Sonora, Guanajuato and Guadalajara. Beyond the vehicles, ropes had been strung between poles dug into the sand. Blue plastic tarpaulins stretched over the ropes to provide a temporary shelter. Tents and pseudo-tents of all colors dotted the usually bare beach. All the doors of one SUV had been opened so that the entire beach population could hear the chant of drum-heavy Salsa and Hard Rock music from its sound system.

For what had to be over a hundred people, there were no sources of fresh water and no toilet facilities at the playa. One enterprising mother was leading her child back into the jungle to add to the brown stained Kleenex paper trail of relief. Enid thought,

"At least that's one dump not going into the ocean!"

The sole garbage drum with its hand-painted *Basura* sign had been dumped over, probably by adventurous dogs. Already overfilled, its contents of plastic bottles, paper and trash-filled multi-colored plastic bags from Gigante and Wal Mart littered the ground. The contrast between this environmental carnage and the beauty of the hibiscus and bougainvillea in her garden was dramatic. Many people excused it all by saying,

"It's their beach. They were here long before us and deserve their vacation pleasures."

Enid felt otherwise. She quickly conceded the rights of the Mexicans on the beach, but could not forgive those others that had publicized and were profiting from the invasion of Santa Rita. Their sin was marketing without also pressuring for adequate controls and sanitary facilities. The hucksters had the power to do good and had failed. She hoped that CAUSE could right some of the wrong.

Over in Punta Viento, Genie wasn't as concerned about Santa Rita as she was about her husband's increasingly distant attitude towards her and their son. She had long accepted his diffidence with others, even his total disregard for the Casa de Mastil owners. Genie was pleased that at least she'd developed new friends that did not know or care about Pedro's developments in Santa Rita. Few had ever been there more than once. Genie could walk Punta Viento streets without acquaintances turning away from even her simplest greeting or attempts to make conversation.

She seldom discussed financial problems with Pedro, unless it was a question of how to pay upcoming school and food bills. Pedro seemed continually preoccupied with unrevealed concerns. When she'd try to start a conversation, he'd immediately turn away to straighten a picture or move a ceramic bowl. Every time she dared to ask him about a new customer or new project he would only give her a name or discuss what they had to eat at a luncheon meeting. Then he would cut the conversation short, building a wall to shut out reality. He didn't share with her the details of the ridiculous lawsuit being reviewed by a panel of judges that accused him of permit violations, bribery and fraud. He knew that the suit was being filed by some tree-hugging lawyer named Chavez from Mexico City. The man obviously didn't understand how the permit system worked in Santa Rita. It was standard procedure to reward a government agent for services rendered. Chavez could only be seeking personal gain. He wanted fame as a crusader that was stopping Santa Rita's inevitable growth and ignoring the benefits that he, Pedro, had showered on the villagers. Pedro learned that the lawsuit was promoted by a group of locals that called their association CAUSE. Pedro's attorney had advised him, as usual, not to discuss the case, not to answer any questions about it to anyone and certainly not to get anything on paper that could back-fire. To avoid any unpleasant contact for him in Santa Rita, he made Imelda drive to Punta Viento each day to provide him with current figures on the hotel income and expenses. While she described the money matters, he walked around the room fingering table pieces and straightening throw rugs.

The Riviera Resort received final planning approval and a permit to start construction on its first phase. The occasion called for a well-publicized groundbreaking ceremony to be followed by a fiesta on the beach. Many of the Mexicans and most of the foreigners turned out in the late afternoon to applaud at first the Governor, then the Mayor of the Ejito and finally the two partners that made ceremonial scoops with a gold-painted shovel to signal the start of the project. The governor spoke about the financial benefits the resort would bring to Santa Rita and the state. The Mayor praised his good friends, *Don Juan* and *Senor Rusti* that were bringing improvements to Santa Rita without spoiling the charm and spirit of this fine coastal community.

After the speeches the crowd moved to the sand where newly-built palapas sheltered a cocktail bar, a small band and a dozen dining tables whose covers suggested white waves splashing in a bright blue sea. A long counter filled with bowls of nachos, salsa, Manchego cheeses, shelled shrimp and guacamole bordered the dining tables. Juan's *guardaespaldas* were filleting Dorado with their fishing knives in preparation for grilling them on the mesquite fire.

The party brought out most of the members of the association and Enid and Ed were surprised to see that even Grant England was there. He must have been back in Santa Rita for the surfing. Enid and Ed sat at a table with Nancy Devereux and the neighbor whose lot line had been invaded by the high-rise. They had discussed the weather, the Riviera, the fishing, the surfing and were vainly trying not to discuss the tower or its developer, when Rusty approached their table and said,

"Hola, Ed. It is so nice to see you here. Your friends also." Rusty and Ed had become friends through a mutual interest in deep-sea fishing. When Ed told him about his boat problems that kept him from casting out any lines, Rusty invited Ed to join him on a fishing trip using one of the skiffs purchased for the new resort. Ed introduced Rusty to the table. Rusty shook hands around the table and sat down next to Enid. Their introductory conversation covered the usual niceties of who they were, where they came from and why they were in Santa Rita. Enid became curious about Rusty's early days in the village and he told her about trading with the Huichols.

"Do you suppose their village is still there?" Enid asked.

"I am sure that by now the government has preserved the area as an historic monument. Those petrographs are too valuable to be left for pilfering or damage."

"Did you and Pedro expand your sales of Huichol artifacts?"

"No, we then opened a restaurant." He then told her about the rough chairs, the fish tacos and Pedro waiting on tables. This last surprised her.

"How could that sphinx have been a greeter for your customers? He never says more than three words to anyone unless they look like hot prospects for a cheating. I asked Pedro and Genie to stop by for a drink when my villa was finished. She couldn't have been nicer, almost as if she'd been liberated. Perhaps it was the wine. Anyway, he of course wouldn't touch alcohol, and sat there with his hands in his lap and the strangest redness in his face, almost as if he was developing a rash and was waiting in the doctor's office for help. I was scared of bringing up any local issues and the furnishing struggle was over, so we had nothing to discuss. The next day I saw him with his arm around a new prospect talking up another deal." Rusty listened politely as Enid described how her invitation was never returned. She was never asked to visit the Sessions. They both laughed a little over Ed's confrontations with the staff. Rusty then got up and said to the others,

"It is a pleasure to meet all of you. If you please, I would like you to meet some of my friends." He soon returned with three other men. One of them was Grant England.

"I'm sure that some of you know Grant. It took a while, but I finally coaxed him back for our ceremony. I'd also like you to meet Jerry and Bob Misrack. You all have a lot in common." He paused and then said, "Oh, before I forget, I'm going to drop Juan and his boys off the point tomorrow so they can snorkel. Ed, if you want to join us, we could go fishing after that."

"I'd like that," Ed replied.

Another table was pulled over to seat the three men. Enid innocently asked what they all might have in common. Grant England started the conversation by describing his original partnership with Pedro. He told how he had traded his shares for what Pedro turned into air space. He said little about the lawsuit except that it had been settled and that the collateral in lieu of a bond was the Sessions' condominium in Punta Viento. Ed reviewed his problems with the boat and his hassles over the storage rooms on level 2 of the tower.

"He sold me the whole floor and then tried to steal half of it back. He cut off my parking space. I hope that they make him tear down the damned building, down to my roof that is!" Jerry Misrack followed with his revelation.

"You should worry. Bob and I each put up sixty thousand for half of level 6. Now we've learned that there's a third party, a dentist, who has put down money for the entire floor; and there's no floor there! When I first met the man I really admired him: those great design ideas and all he'd done for the community; or at least what he said he'd done. We went surfing and played tennis." Jerry continued, "When he told me there might be a short delay in Santa Rita, no problem just Mexico, I was happy to put money into his new Punta Viento villa. We were sure to make a killing when it was sold. Now that he's living there, we'll never be able to move it because he always comes up with a reason not to show the place. My only compensation is that they have to move out whenever I want to use the place."

"So, we are all here," said Enid. "This is the Hate Pedro Society: Rusty, Grant, Me, Ed, and now Bob and Jerry."

"I'll bet there are more," Ed said.

"If this was Chicago, he wouldn't be alive," chipped in Jerry.

Pedro was one of the few townspeople that didn't show up for the ceremony. He'd heard that Juan and Rusty were listening to the association complaints and lowering the density of their project. Pedro wanted to avoid his former friends for obvious reasons but also because he didn't want to give credence to a project that he knew was going to be direct competition for Casa de Mastil. He tried to hide his worries with the derisive thought that no one would want to stay in a former sewer plant. He avoided speaking out loud his secret name for the proposed resort: *La Casa de Mierda*.

This was the often strange, but consistent dichotomy of the two Peter Oliver Sessions. On the one hand the simple surfer turned evangelical convert would not utter a swear word. On the other hand, the surfer turned hotelier was a ruthless businessperson. He shrugged off lawsuits. He refused to hear complaints about his cost cutting from villa owners, but lavish spending wherever it suited Pedro. He had stolen land from a neighbor and was stealing water from another neighbor's reservoir. He had defied the county, state and federal governments. Yet he never, ever would describe his competition as the House of Shit.

24

Peter Oliver Sessions finally had a copy in his hands of the action filed by Chavez for CAUSE. The *Denuncia* or complaint had to be reviewed by a number of government agencies before becoming official, giving Pedro and his attorney time to consider possible actions. He had already cut off two floors of the tower and believed that that would answer any possible action by the government or the courts. The extent of the CAUSE complaint gave him further reasons to worry. The long document stated these facts.

A.1: November 1988—A project called Ecoturistico Casa de Mastils was to be constructed in the community of Vista Mar.

A.2: February, 1989—The Office of the Federal Environmental Prosecutor (PROFEPA) in Sinaloa signed an evaluation that considered the project legitimate in every way.

A.3: March, 1989—The Director General of Urban Development declared Casa de Mastils illegal because it did not follow the zoning and planning laws of the State of Sinaloa.

A.5: By November 1990, Peter and Eugenia Sessions were working illegally for at least two years on a project with a similar name to Casa de Mastils, in Vista Mar, but the actual project was in the community of Santa Rita. They did not have the required evaluation and authorization for the Environmental Impact (Manifestation de Impacto Ambiental)

A.6: April, 1991—The Board of Defense of the Pacific Coast, while investigating a complaint of water pollution, discovered that parts of Casa de Mastils (the tower) had illegally encroached on Federal lands.

A.7: June, 1992—PROFEPA makes an inspection and finds illegal excavation for the tower. They issue a Temporary Suspension order.

A8: August, 1992—PROFEPA inspects the site and finds the Suspension order has not been followed.

A.9: September, 1992—PROFEPA in Sinaloa issued an Agreement of Inspection certifying that Casa de Mastils was actually in Santa Rita, not Vista Mar. Because the tower was at least 56% constructed and had removed large parts of the hill, an Environmental Impact report was impossible. They therefore required TOTAL SUSPENSION of any further construction.

A.10: Access: The construction of the tower impedes access to the Playa de los Muertos.

A.11: February, 1991—Sessions submitted a report of Environmental Impact for an ocean front development of 8 villas, 3 stories high.

A.12: To present—Sessions has continually ignored orders to stop the work.

Pedro read a clause that followed these citations that described the CAUSE request that the tower be reduced in height to three stories. CAUSE wanted to knock down a unit that was already built, paid for and occupied on level 5! He had a legal right to 6 stories! He also read the charge that the tower was built in the Federal Zone. He was convinced all the charges were ridiculous and could be answered.

His solution was to order his attorney to immediately start a process that he hoped would throw all the problems with the tower, and the rest of Casa de Mastil, back on the owners. He would speed up the creation of that Condominium Regime. This might not only throw all the legal problems back at the owners and get him off the hook but it could silence their complaints about construction. This might also get Enid out of his hair. She had been harassing him with requests for Regularization and a Condominium Regime. She would now understand that he wanted the process completed as much as they did.

The hotel properties consisted of two or more parcels. The parcel that he had stolen from Grant England, and upon which he was building the tower, had actually been Regularized before Grant bought it. The other parcels were variously held in the name of Eugenia Sessions or Isabella Eugenia de Sessions. Pedro's first move was to get approval in Mexico City to combine all of the parcels and place them in a bank trust with Mexican citizen Genie as the beneficiary. He then turned over his engineering survey, the one that took back half of the floor that Ed thought he bought, so an attorney could legally describe them. The attorney then had to draw up documents that would define the covenants and codes for a condominium association.

Pedro wanted to complete the process as soon as possible. He would then thrust the scheme onto all the villa owners and give them a minimal deadline for review and approval. If they didn't approve, they would lose out on the opportunity to obtain a legal title. Behind this haste was his knowledge that he could be seriously sued by both the owners and the government. He knew he could be fined and possibly jailed for all the permit evasions as well as the errors and omissions in the tower construction. With the condo he hoped to dump all the problems onto the owners so that he and Genie would be free to live peacefully in Punta Viento.

This grand plan was scarred by a simple line drawn on a map that defined the pristine Federal Zone as "all that land between the mean high tide line and a point thirty meters inshore within which no structure or other improvement is allowed." The surveyor told Pedro what he already knew: many of the units actually had areas that sat within the Federal Zone. The attorney proposed an answer to the Federal Zone problem. Pedro should have Genie, as a Mexican, apply for a permit to temporarily occupy the zone. Others had used the device to place temporary food and umbrella palapas on the sand. With the permit, Genie would in turn rent back the parts of the units that the owners thought they'd already bought and owned.

Pedro was thinking about the lawsuit as he sat down on a silk-covered sofa in his living area. He looked down at the cushions and saw that he'd rumpled them. The sight made him quickly jump up, smooth over the cushion and move to a hard-seated side chair. Next to the chair was a table with a single glass globe sitting in its middle. He gazed at the swirls of color within the globe and then reached out to carefully caress the cold surface. The globe moved slightly, so he moved it back to its original position. The globe was perfection. He pondered his options as he slowly removed his hand from the globe. He knew how his life could still be perfection. He had to keep playing a waiting game. Lawsuits could be delayed and judges' decisions could be appealed. Elections could put the outside party back in power. His old friends would regain their seats and business could be done as usual. He could re-build the levels of the tower. He had saved most of the construction materials. This would satisfy the two guys that he'd pre-sold level 6. The third guy could have level 7. He could pay off Grant England and get back his condo in Punta Viento. He'd do anything but move out of the house they now occupied. This was his house of order where everything stayed where he wanted it to be. This was his idea of *paraiso*.

His euphoria was short-lived, as he began to think of all the bad things that could happen to him. What could stop the condo regime? There was Ed Seifert; but he had to join the regime to get a clear title. Unlike Enid, Ed was just sold air space in a building. Enid? Enid was his worst critic. She has been bothering him ever since La Arboleda was built and she'd already asked dozens of questions about how the regime would affect her. He wondered for a few minutes about how to silence her and then had an idea.

Pedro realized that he could get rid of Enid's obvious objections to his condo idea. He could just separate her out of the condominium regime. Enid had the rights to the land and was the only owner with direct access to a public way. Once Enid knew that she could have her own clear title, she would never raise a voice against the condo idea. Of course he was right. He called Imelda to suggest to Enid in an off-hand manner that having her own subdivided lot was possible.

Enid took a while to absorb the idea. Why was he doing this? How could he make such a generous offer when she was attacking him on all sides? Perhaps Pedro was so introverted that he knew little about the makeup of the association, and didn't want to know anything about his adversaries. Perhaps it was Genie. Perhaps it was a religious moment. Enid walked down the stairs to share this information with Ed. He welcomed her at the door and they walked to seats on his deck. Enid felt bad rejoicing about independence when the one person that disliked Pedro more than she couldn't get that. Ed had a different attitude.

"I will come out of this somehow; and, besides, I sort of enjoy fighting the man. What impresses me is how you have beaten him down with the association that you founded and your own refusal to be pushed around. You once told me that you were named after Enide, the unfortunate wife. For my money you've done enough here in Santa Rita to compensate for all the battering that Enides got in the past." She smiled at the compliment, wondering where he picked up the weird reference.

When the papers were completed for transferring Enid's property, Pedro and Genie had to once again go back to Santa Rita to sign them to complete the transaction. He first drove into Mazatlan to rent an SUV with dark tinted windows all around. Then he and Genie drove back to the town whose citizens first welcomed them and now would stone their vehicle if they recognized the occupants. Pedro had called ahead to reserve the Casa Canto for a night's stay. As they entered their driveway, they could see the large palapa, still tied to its brick platform, framed between mature palm trees.

When Genie went into their old bedroom for a mid-day nap, Pedro stayed on the porch, stroking the carefully steamed crease in his linen shorts. He watched the surfers wait for the best waves and then head safely into shore without mishaps. Much as he wanted to have his life go on catching the best waves and avoiding pitfalls, he begrudgingly admitted that the analogy didn't always work. He'd always been able to ride the best waves and, when off the water, build up his mental walls. His coming concession to separate Enid from the hotel property was a sign of weakness. Although by agreement she held all the rights, Pedro had always considered La Arboleda as part of his domain. Its loss was just the start of a dozen bad waves that he had to ride and the crumbling of all the walls he'd built up over a lifetime. Surely, his work had been beneficial. Surely his Sunday prayers had been heard.

Another voice told him that all the prayers and all the good works could not save him. He didn't have the money to pay off Grant England. They would never get back their condo. The villa in Punta Viento would be taken away from him. The Sessions would be kicked out of their borrowed palace in a gated subdivision. The minute that tower owners were melded into the condominium regime, there would be twenty lawsuits. When the ones unlucky enough to be in the Federal Zone learned that they were renting pieces from Genie, there would be ten additional lawsuits. Then there were county, state and federal employees that were involved in the illegal permit process. He could hope that the men he'd given gratuities were inaccessible, on long vacations or no longer there to be prosecuted. PROFEPA? CAUSE? FEDERAL ZONE? Where did they all suddenly come from?

Being back at the Casa Canto (he hated the derisive term Casa de Cabra) gave him some kind of comfort. He walked along the deck. He touched and stroked the smooth concrete pillars shaped to look like palm tree trunks. He ran a finger along the shiny enameled frame of the white shutters. He stopped at a solid paneled door set into the wall behind the deck. He reached to the top of the large molding that surrounded the door and groped through a layer of dust. Yes, the key was still there. He retrieved it and then unlocked and opened the door to a storeroom that he'd almost forgotten existed.

In the light thrown into the open doorway, he could make out a broken chair that he'd told Genie he'd repair. He saw a shelf that held two woven baskets that they'd used to soften the glare of hanging light bulbs. A pillow with *Genie* embroidered into the satin cloth was propped up against the wall. Two plastic storage boxes held long-forgotten artifacts made by the Huichols. A small, once green, rusting metal case stood beside the boxes. Leaning against the rear wall was a well-scarred Jeff Ho Zephyr surf board.

Pedro touched the pillow that he'd bought the first week that they arrived in Santa Rita. He then hesitated, but gingerly picked up the metal case and carried it out on the deck. He put the case on a low table and put thumbs and forefingers over the two hasps. The box hinge squeaked as he opened the top to see something that he hadn't been near since his marriage. Carefully wrapped in a small plastic bag were matches, papers and enough Acapulco Gold to soothe even the most addicted victim. It was still there from the days of sharing the palapa with Rusty and all the others that drifted in and out of town.

Whether from curiosity or instinct, Pedro rolled a reefer from the contents and lit up. The calming sensation was exactly what he needed to wipe away his troubles. His thoughts were carried back to his first years in Santa Rita. He could feel FREEDOM: Freedom from the draft, freedom from his father, freedom to surf and freedom to build whatever and wherever he pleased. He even sensed a freedom from the guilt he felt every time that he prayed for an undeserved forgiveness. He was free from the hesitant doubts he had whenever he used Genie's name to legalize his property scams. He was free from Enid Williams, free from Grant England and he imagined himself crushing big foam core letters from the alphabet that spelled out PROFEPA. There was a way to be free from all that forever.

Pedro was free to find refuge where he had always found refuge. He put on his trunks, shed his Hawaiian shirt, pulled the straps tight on his sandals, got out the Jeff Ho board and headed for the surf. At the last minute he decided to take the route through the cemetery and take off from Playa los Muertos. There the cove was crystal clear and as he paddled out from the beach he could see schools of small bait fish under his board.

As he headed around the point, he noticed two men in a boat that was idling on his left about a quarter of a mile offshore. They may have had fishing lines out, but it looked more as if they'd just dropped off some skin divers. There were three snorkels slowly moving above the hidden reef on his right. Two were men with white tee shirts held to their waists with web belts. He saw one of them pull out a knife to spear a fish below. A third man that he thought he recognized started to head back to shore while the first two headed out on a line that would cross Pedro's path. Pedro Sessions pointed his board towards the open sea between the boat and the two divers.

25

Rubble rock fingers of land reached out to embrace the mile long Santa Rita beach. Waves that were born far out in the Pacific rolled over the gently sloping sands whose multiple grains had drifted south from Mazatlan, the Sea of Cortez and points north in California. The waves continually rearranged the landform but they also provided the natural forces to push Santa Rita's fleet of open skiffs up on the sand. The waves were god-sent locomotion for the fishermen who formed the backbone of this small Mexican *pueblo*.

Santa Ritans watched each morning for the arrival of the boats so that they could move from fisherman to fisherman to assess the previous night's catch. The residents were usually dispersed amongst the many skiffs to look and paw and bargain for the best *pesca*, but today they were concentrated around a single boat. Their typical purchasing zeal had been replaced by a concentrated curiosity. They were looking at a very dead body that had been placed on top of the day's catch of dorado, red snapper and ocean shrimp.

Beside the body was an ancient but recently used Jeff Ho Zephyr surfboard.

978-0-595-39451-7
0-595-39451-5

Printed in the United States
84721LV00003B/90/A

9 780595 394517